science

animals

food

In·Focus

英語閱讀
活用五大關鍵技巧

4

作者 | Owain Mckimm / Zachary Fillingham / Laura Phelps / Richard Luhrs
譯者 | 劉嘉珮／丁宥暄
審訂 | Richard Luhrs

MP3
寂天雲 APP

如何下載 MP3 音檔

❶ 寂天雲 APP 聆聽：掃描書上 QR Code 下載「寂天雲－英日語學習隨身聽」APP。加入會員後，用 APP 內建掃描器再次掃描書上 QR Code，即可使用 APP 聆聽音檔。

❷ 官網下載音檔：請上「寂天閱讀網」（www.icosmos.com.tw），註冊會員／登入後，搜尋本書，進入本書頁面，點選「MP3 下載」下載音檔，存於電腦等其他播放器聆聽使用。

Contents Chart 目錄

| | Introduction 簡介 | | 06 |
| | How Do I Use This Book? 使用導覽 | | 10 |

	Article Title 文章標題	Article Type 文章體裁 Subject 主題	Page 頁碼
1	Inner Beauty 內在美	instant message 簡訊 Teens 青少年生活	12
2	Yang Family Budget 楊家的預算計畫	pie chart 圓餅圖 Finance/Economics 金融／經濟	14
3	Taking to the Skies 登上高空	blog 部落格 Internet or Technology 網路或科技	16
4	Going Through Customs 過海關	dialogue 對話 Daily Routines 日常生活	18
5	Clinic Schedule 門診時間表	table 表格 Health & Body 健康與身體	20
6	Get Well Card 慰問卡	card 卡片 Friends & Personal Relationships 友情與愛情	22
7	Take Lemons and Make Lemonade 化逆境為動力	interview 訪談 Teens 青少年生活	24
8	Take Me Out to the Ball Game 帶我去看球賽	bar graph 柱狀圖 Sports 體育	26
9	Everyone's a Movie Critic 大家都能是影評	forum 討論區 Entertainment 娛樂	28
10	You Can't Park Here 請勿停車	note 便條 Daily Routines 日常生活	30
11	St. Patrick's Day Parade 聖派屈克節遊行	map 地圖 Holidays & Festivals 節日與節慶	32

Article Title 文章標題	Article Type 文章體裁 Subject 主題	Page 頁碼
12 Courage 勇氣	poem 詩 Arts & Literature 藝術與文學	34
13 Save Our Park 搶救我們的公園	brochure/leaflet 小冊子／宣傳單 Daily Routines 日常生活	36
14 School Talent Show 校園才藝表演	dialogue 對話 School 學校	38
15 The Street Store 街頭捐贈商店	double passages 雙短文 Inspiration 勵志	40
16 Some Timely Inspiration 及時的啟發	postcard 明信片 Inspiration 勵志	42
17 Hi, I'm Tony. I'm Looking for . . . 網路徵友	website 網站 Friends & Personal Relationships 友情與愛情	44
18 Graduation 畢業典禮	diary 日記 School 學校	46
19 A Special Evening 別出心裁的一晚	table 表格 Friends & Personal Relationships 友情與愛情	48
20 Survival Camp 荒野求生訓練營	poster 海報 Entertainment 娛樂	50
21 My Boss's Busy Schedule 我上司的忙碌行程	calendar 行事曆 Business 商務	52
22 Recipe of the Week: Panda Bear Cookies 本週食譜：熊貓餅乾	recipe 食譜 Food 食物	54
23 New Planet Discovered 發現新行星	news clip 新聞影片 Science 科學	56
24 Everything Must Go 清倉大拍賣	note/notice 公告 Life/Everyday Life 生活／日常生活	58
25 Living Murphy's Law 實現莫非定律	passage 短文 Psychology 心理	60
26 Wedding Invitation 結婚喜帖	card 卡片 Life/Everyday Life 生活／日常生活	62

	Article Title 文章標題	Article Type 文章體裁 Subject 主題	Page 頁碼
27	**Tips for Learning English** 學好英文的小撇步	passage + bullet points 短文＋條列式重點 Education 教育	64
28	**A Message for the Future** 送到未來的訊息	note 便條 Life/Everyday Life 生活／日常生活	66
29	**Just Ask Lina** 琳娜萬事通	questionnaire 問卷 Internet or Technology 網路或科技	68
30	**Our Planet Is Heating Up** 地球正在持續升溫中	line graph 折線圖 Environment & Conservation 環境保育	70
31	***The Wave That Changed Art*** 《顛覆藝術界的浪花》	book foreword 書序 Arts & Literature 藝術與文學	72
32	**Head Transplants** 頭部移植	Q & A 問與答 Science 科學	74
33	**Schools in Finland: The Secret of Their Success** 芬蘭學校的成功秘訣	passage 短文 Education 教育	76
34	**How to Do Sit-Ups** 仰臥起坐的做法	instruction 教學 Sports 體育	78
35	***A Brief History of Canada*** 《加拿大簡史》	index 索引 School 學校	80
36	**Soak Up Some Japanese Culture** 浸淫日本文化	passage + bullet points 短文＋條列式重點 Culture 文化	82
37	**A Cappella Competition** 無伴奏合唱大賽	broadcasting 廣播 Entertainment 娛樂	84
38	**George Psalmanazar: The Fake Formosan** 喬治‧撒瑪納札：偽福爾摩沙人	passage 短文 Famous or Interesting People 著名或有趣人物	86

	Article Title 文章標題	Article Type 文章體裁 / Subject 主題	Page 頁碼
39	**Finding the Perfect Home** 尋覓完美住宅	advertisement 廣告 / Finance/Economics 金融／經濟	88
40	**TV Planet: Program Guide for Friday, 6ᵗʰ September** 電視星球：9月6日星期五 節目指南	table 表格 / Entertainment 娛樂	90
41	**You Got In** 錄取通知	email 電子郵件 / School 學校	92
42	**Vote for Sam** 投票給山姆	pamphlet 小冊子 / Politics 政治	94
43	**The Whole Is Greater Than Its Parts** 全貌優於細節：馬賽克藝術	passage 短文 / Arts & Literature 藝術與文學	96
44	**A Spiritual Journey** 心靈旅程：瑜珈之美	table of contents 目錄 / Health & Body 健康與身體	98
45	*Mikania Micrantha—Invader!* 外來入侵種「小花蔓澤蘭」	column 專欄 / Plants 植物	100
46	**SARS and MERS, Meet the WHO** 淺談 SARS、MERS 和世界衛生組織	newspaper 報紙 / Health & Body 健康與身體	102
47	**Smog: Choking the World's Cities** 霧霾：令城市呼吸困難的公害	magazine article 雜誌文章 / Environment & Conservation 環境保育	104
48	**Chen Cheng Po** 台灣畫家陳澄波	passage 短文 / Arts & Literature 藝術與文學	106
49	**The Dogs of War** 軍犬創傷症候群	news clip 新聞影片 / Animals 動物	108
50	**A Green Skyline** 綠色天際線	passage 短文 / Environment & Conservation 環境保育	110

中譯 —— 112
解答 —— 143

Introduction 簡介

　　本套書依程度共分四冊,專為初中級讀者編寫。每冊包含50篇閱讀文章、30餘種文體與題材。各冊分級主要針對文章字數多寡、字級難易度、文法深淺、句子長度來區分。生活化的主題配合多元化的體裁,讓讀者透過教材,體驗豐富多樣的語言學習經驗,提昇學習興趣,增進學習效果。

字數 (每篇)	國中 1200 單字(每篇)	國中 1201- 2000 單字 (每篇)	高中 7000 (3, 4, 5 級) (每篇)	文法程度	句子長度
Book 1 120–150	93%	7 字	3 字	(國一) first year	15 字
Book 2 150–180	86%	15 字	6 字	(國二) second year	18 字
Book 3 180–210	82%	30 字	7 字	(國三) third year	25 字
Book 4 210–250	75%	50 字	12 字	(國三進階) advanced	28 字

本書架構
閱讀文章

　　本套書涵蓋豐富且多元的主題與體裁。文章形式廣泛蒐羅各類生活中常見的實用體裁，包含短文、簡訊、部落格、卡片、訪談、詩、食譜等三十餘種，以日常相關的生活經驗為重點編寫設計，幫助加強基礎閱讀能力，提升基本英語溝通能力，為基礎生活英語紮根。

　　收錄大量題材有趣、多元且生活化的短文，範圍囊括青少年生活、勵志、健康與身體、藝術與文學、環境保育、網路或科技、心理、文化、商業、科學、政治等三十餘種，主題多元化且貼近生活經驗，可激起學生學習興趣，協助學生理解不同領域知識。

閱讀測驗

　　每篇短文後，皆接有五題閱讀理解選擇題，評量學生對文章的理解程度。閱讀測驗所訓練學生的閱讀技巧包括：

文章中心思想
（Main Idea）／
主題（Subject Matter）

支持性細節
（Supporting Details）

從上下文猜測字義
（Words in Context）

文意推論
（Making Inferences）

看懂影像圖表
（Visualizing
Comprehension）

文章中心思想（Main Idea）

閱讀文章時，讀者可以試著問自己：「**作者想要傳達什麼訊息？**」透過審視理解的方式，檢視自己是否了解文章意義。

文章主題（Subject Matter）

這類問題幫助讀者專注在所閱讀的文章中，在閱讀文章前幾行後，讀者應該問自己：「**這篇文章是關於什麼？**」這麼做能幫助你立刻集中注意力，快速理解文章內容，進而掌握整篇文章脈絡。

支持性細節（Supporting Details）

每篇文章都是由細節組成來支持主題句。「**支持性細節**」包括範例、說明、敘述、定義、比較、對比和比喻。

從上下文猜測字義（Words in Context）

由上下文猜生字意義，是英文閱讀中一項很重要的策略。弄錯關鍵字詞的意思會導致誤解作者想要傳達的觀點。

文意推論（Making Inferences）

推論性的問題會要讀者歸納文章中已有的資訊，來思考、推理，並且將線索連結起來，推論可能的事實，這種問題的目的是訓練讀者的批判性思考和邏輯性。

看懂影像圖表（Visualizing Comprehension）

這類問題考驗讀者理解視覺資料的能力，包括表格、圖片、地圖等，或是索引、字典，學會運用這些圖像資料能增進你對文章的整體理解。

How Do I Use This Book? 使用導覽

主題多元化

題材有趣且多元，貼近日常生活經驗，包含青少年生活、勵志、健康與身體、藝術與文學、環境保育、網路或科技、科學等，激發學生學習興趣，協助學生理解不同領域知識。

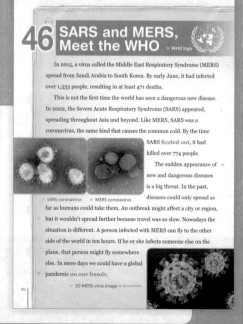

體裁多樣化

廣納生活中常見的實用體裁，包含短文、簡訊、部落格、卡片、訪談、詩、食譜等，以日常相關生活經驗設計編寫，為基礎生活英語紮根。

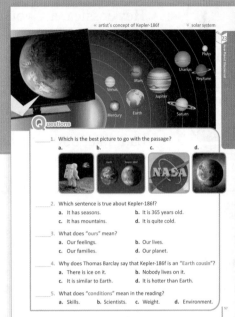

閱讀技巧練習題

左頁文章、右頁測驗的設計方式，短文後皆接有五題閱讀理解選擇題，評量學生對文章的理解程度，訓練五大閱讀技巧。

19 A Special Evening

John and Silvia celebrated their first anniversary by eating out at one of the city's most exclusive French restaurants. It was a lovely evening. Silvia was dressed to the nines, and John had an opportunity to order his favorite dessert. They had such a great time that they didn't even care about how expensive the meal was. Here is their order, and a poster advertising the restaurant.

豐富多彩的圖表

運用大量彩色圖表與圖解，搭配文章輕鬆學習，以視覺輔助記憶，學習成效加倍。

1 Inner Beauty

Beth: Hey Jessica, are you there?

Jessica: Sure I am. What's up?

Beth: I just got into a big fight with my mom. It was pretty bad; like, both of us really **took the gloves off**.

5 **Jessica:** That's awful! What were you guys fighting about?

Beth: It was the same old story. She caught me trying to leave the house wearing makeup. I was almost out the back door when she called me back inside. Then she saw my eyeliner and totally **flipped out**.

10 **Jess:** I can imagine, especially after what happened last weekend.

Beth: She's out of her mind on this. I'm 14 years old. That's almost an adult. I mean, take you, for example. Your mom has let you wear makeup since you were 12.

Jess: True, but have you noticed that I almost never put it on?

Beth: Actually, I *have* noticed. What's the deal with 15 that? If my mom were that cool, I'd wear makeup all the time.

Jess: I can see how makeup would seem like a big deal if everyone were using it except you. 20 But there's really nothing exciting about it. In fact, it's kind of a pain in the neck.

Beth: What do you mean?

⌃ eyeliner

« wear makeup

Putting makeup on and taking it off takes a lot of time. And we shouldn't

25 need to wear makeup to feel beautiful. **Jessica** That comes from inside. It's about what kind of person you are.

Well said! So does this mean I can have your makeup?

Beth

1

Inner Beauty

Questions

_____ 1. What is Jessica trying to say in the reading?
  a. It is too much trouble to put on makeup.
  b. Makeup makes you a good person.
  c. Inner beauty is what really counts.
  d. Beth's mom isn't being fair.

_____ 2. When was Jessica first allowed to wear makeup?
  a. When she was 14.　　 b. When she was 12.
  c. When she turned 18.　 d. When she started middle school.

_____ 3. What does it mean that Beth and her mom "**took the gloves off**"?
  a. They cleaned up the house together.
  b. They forgave each other.
  c. They ignored each other.
  d. They argued and didn't hold back.

_____ 4. Which of the following probably happened to Beth last weekend?
  a. Her mom warned her not to wear makeup.
  b. She went to the mall with Jessica.
  c. Her mom came home after a long holiday.
  d. She had a party for her mom's birthday.

_____ 5. What does it mean that Beth's mom "**flipped out**"?
  a. She jumped in the air.　 b. She started to cry.
  c. She didn't say anything.　 d. She became very angry.

2 Yang Family Budget

« savir

Drawing up a budget can be a great way to get your family's finances in order. Take the Yang family for example. Mr. Yang didn't like the idea of a budget to begin with; "I'd rather go to the dentist," he said. However, when Mrs. Yang cam

5 up with a goal the whole family could agree on, Mr. Yang changed hi mind. That goal was saving up for a new apartment, one where each of the Yangs' children could have his or her own bedroom.

The Yangs began by simply writing down what they spent their money on. This is a good first step in any budget, because it helps

10 determine where your money goes. Once you know what you're already spending money on, you can make a budget for next month. The Yangs have been building their **nest egg** for years now, and soon they'll be able to buy that bigger apartment.

⌃ gasoline ⌃ mobile phone ⌃ entertainment ⌃ eating out

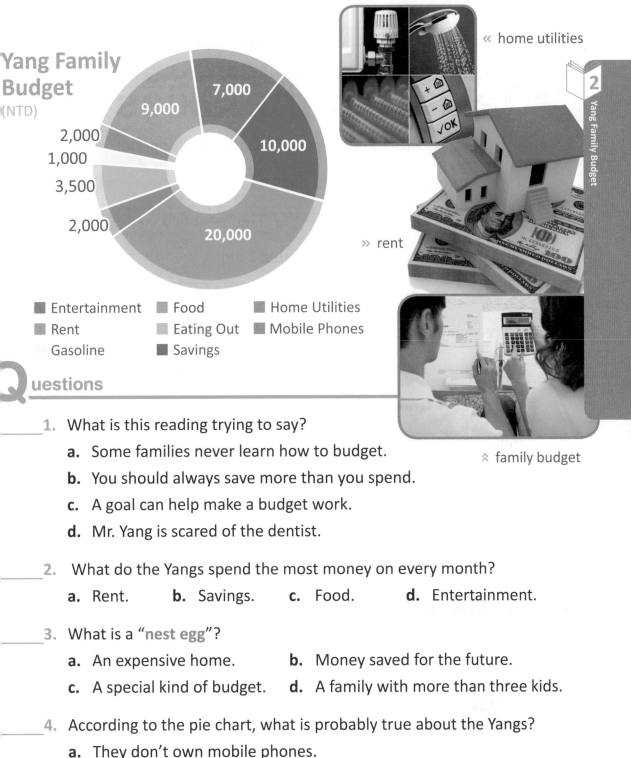

Yang Family Budget
(NTD)

7,000
9,000
2,000
1,000
3,500
2,000
10,000
20,000

« home utilities

» rent

- Entertainment
- Rent
- Gasoline
- Food
- Eating Out
- Savings
- Home Utilities
- Mobile Phones

Questions

_____ 1. What is this reading trying to say?
   a. Some families never learn how to budget.
   b. You should always save more than you spend.
   c. A goal can help make a budget work.
   d. Mr. Yang is scared of the dentist.

☆ family budget

_____ 2. What do the Yangs spend the most money on every month?
   a. Rent.   **b.** Savings.   **c.** Food.   **d.** Entertainment.

_____ 3. What is a "**nest egg**"?
   a. An expensive home.   **b.** Money saved for the future.
   c. A special kind of budget.   **d.** A family with more than three kids.

_____ 4. According to the pie chart, what is probably true about the Yangs?
   a. They don't own mobile phones.
   b. They do not own their apartment.
   c. They don't own a car or a motorcycle.
   d. They take lots of vacations.

_____ 5. Which of the following do the Yangs spend the least amount of money on?
   a. Home Utilities.   **b.** Food.   **c.** Entertainment.   **d.** Gasoline.

3 Taking to the Skies

Today's posting might seem a bit **out of place**, but bear with me. I was having lunch the other day and I heard someone talking about unmanned aerial vehicles (UAVs). They sounded cool so I decided to check them out. Am I ever glad that I did!

5　　Here's the deal: UAVs are flying machines that don't have pilots. They include large, military-grade UAVs, like the drones used by the US military. These are the ones that can launch missiles and blow up buildings. We don't like those. Small UAVs, or "personal drones," are much better. These can be put to more peaceful uses. For example, you 10 can put a camera on a personal drone and take pictures from high up in the sky. Or maybe you just want to control a flying robot; that's cool in itself. People say that using a remote control to fly a UAV is more fun

6-Axis CX-20
2.4GHz Similar DJI Phantom 2 vision

●HK-TF2932

⌃ Phantom (UAV)

Questions

_____ 1. What is this blog post about?
- **a.** A pilot.
- **b.** A new camera.
- **c.** Flying machines.
- **d.** The Phantom.

_____ 2. What does the writer not like about the Phantom?
- **a.** It has too few propellers.
- **b.** It launches missiles.
- **c.** The camera is not in the right place.
- **d.** The battery doesn't last long enough.

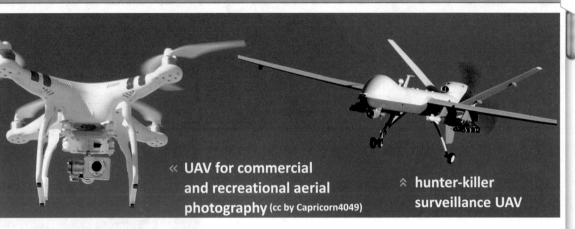

« UAV for commercial and recreational aerial photography (cc by Capricorn4049)

≫ hunter-killer surveillance UAV

than any video game out there.

UAVs are still expensive, but I think I'm going to **jump in**. There

15 is one model that I have my eye on. It's called the Phantom, and it's

got four little propellers on top and a camera on the bottom. One

thing I don't like is the battery. It only lasts 15 minutes and takes a

full hour to recharge.

What do you think, readers? Aren't UAVs great? Should I buy one?

20 Please post your comments below!

_____ 3. What does it mean when something is "**out of place**"?

    a. It does not belong there.   **b.** It is very important.

    c. It is brand new.   **d.** It will change people's minds.

_____ 4. What does the writer mean by "**jump in**"?

    a. He's going to buy a UAV.   **b.** He's going to make his own UAV.

    c. He's going to play videogames.   **d.** He's going to write more blog posts.

_____ 5. Which of the following could be a comment on this blog post?

    a. "Congratulations! After all of your hard work, you deserve it."

    b. "I think the one in the middle is the cutest by far."

    c. "Those things are awesome. I know what I'm saving up for now."

    d. "I think the first film is better than the second by far."

4 Going Through Customs

C Customs Officer   **T** Tourist

C : Good afternoon, sir.
Where are you arriving from today?

T : From Bangkok.

C : I see. Do you have the customs
form you were given on the plane?

T : Yes. Here it is.

C : Thank you, sir. "Nothing to declare."
Could you open your suitcase for me, please?

⌃ Customs

T : All right . . . There you go.

C : Thank you, sir. Did you purchase any of
these items in Thailand?

T : Just these tee-shirts and souvenirs.
They're gifts for friends. Is there any problem?

⌃ X-ray scanner and r
detector at airport
security checkpoint

C : No, these are small items. Did you make
any larger purchases on your trip? Any gold or jewels?

T : Certainly not.
That sort of stuff is way out of my budget!

≫ suitcase

C : What about fruit or other foods?

T : Only this package of coffee you've already seen.

C : That's fine.
Could you open your carry-on bag for me, please?

T : Do I have to? People are waiting for me outside.

C : I'm afraid it's necessary, sir. It won't take long.

T : Okay. There.

C : . . . Uh, what is this, sir? 25

T : Just some sticky rice. I bought it at the market this morning before I flew out. I'd forgotten about it, actually.

C : Mmm. Well, you can't bring this into Taiwan. It's not sealed.

T : Are you sure? It's just one little thing.

C : Sorry, sir; it'll have to stay here with me. Everything else 30 looks fine, however, so you can go now.

T : Thanks. Enjoy my sticky rice!

Questions

1. What could be another title for this reading?
   a. My Holiday in Bangkok
   b. A Visit to the Market
   c. Shopping for Souvenirs
   d. Having Your Bags Checked

2. Where does this conversation take place?
   a. At an airport in Thailand.
   b. At an airport in Taiwan.
   c. At a souvenir shop in Thailand.
   d. At a morning market in Taiwan.

3. Why doesn't the tourist want to open his carry-on bag?
   a. Because he's in a hurry.
   b. Because there's sticky rice inside.
   c. Because it's hard to open.
   d. Because it's getting late.

4. What does the tourist mean when he says, "That sort of stuff is way out of my budget"?
   a. It's too expensive for him.
   b. It's not nice enough for him.
   c. He doesn't know what it is.
   d. He already gave it away.

5. Which of these items was left with the customs officer?
   a. **b.** **c.** **d.**

« Taiwan health insurance IC/smart card

» examine

5 Clinic Schedule

Welcome to the Sunny Creek walk-in clinic. We operate five day a week, and strive to always have two doctors on-site to serve you. Our team of four doctors has over 90 years of combined experience We also offer house calls **in a pinch**. However, please make sure

5   your insurance covers these services before putting a call in.

Below you will find a chart of our doctors' office hours. Althougl we accept walk-in patients, we still encourage you to call ahead and make an appointment for best results.

Questions

_____1.   What is this reading about?

   a. Doctors.   **b.** Days of the week.

   c. A clinic.   **d.** An appointment.

_____2.   John went to see the doctor on Monday morning. After checking his ea the doctor told him to come back on Tuesday afternoon. John said he couldn't because he had to work. The doctor then suggested Wednesd afternoon, and that worked for John. Which doctor did John see?

   a. Dr. Johnson.   **b.** Dr. Roy.   **c.** Dr. Lee.   **d.** Dr. Ivanov.

_____3.   What does "**in a pinch**" mean?

   a. In a car.   **b.** In a bad situation.

   c. In silence.   **d.** In a long time.

		Johnson (Room 101)	Roy (Room 102)	Lee (Room 205)	Ivanov (Room 206)
Monday	Morning		●		●
	Afternoon	●	●	●	
	Evening				
Tuesday	Morning	●	●		
	Afternoon		●	●	●
	Evening				●
Wednesday	Morning	●	●		
	Afternoon		●	●	●
	Evening				●
Thursday	Morning				●
	Afternoon	●		●	●
	Evening				●
Friday	Morning				
	Afternoon	●		●	
	Evening				

Clinic hours: 8:00 – 12:30; 14:30 – 17:30; 18:30 – 22:00

» reception counter

_____ 4. Which of the following is probably true?

    a. Dr. Ivanov likes to work overtime.

    b. Dr. Roy is on vacation.

    c. Dr. Lee has yoga classes on Friday evening.

    d. Dr. Johnson doesn't like to work at night.

_____ 5. Julie made an appointment to see Dr. Ivanov on the morning of August 3, but when she got to the clinic, the secretary said that Dr. Ivanov had left early because his son was sick. Julie could still be seen that morning, but it would have to be by Dr. Johnson. What day of the week was August 3?

    a. Monday.   **b.** Tuesday.   **c.** Wednesday.   **d.** Thursday.

6 Get Well Card

July 6th, 2016

Dear Kathy,

How are you?! I can't tell you how scared I was when I heard what had happened to you. I'm still really concerned, of course, but I'm
5 glad you weren't injured even more seriously. I visited you yesterday morning, but you were still asleep and the nurse told me not to wake you up. I left a small gift for you, which I guess you've seen by now. I hope you like it; I know Snoopy is your favorite cartoon character.

Anyway, we all miss you like crazy, but me most of all. School just
10 isn't any fun without your jokes and gossip, and after I get home I don't feel like doing anything. What's the point if my best friend isn't around? Our family is still going to the beach on Saturday, but I'm sure I'll have a terrible time without you there. We were looking forward to it so much, and then this happened. Mom and Dad have
15 been asking about you every day; they're very sorry you can't join us.

Well, I'm running out of space, so I guess I'll have to go. I swear I'll visit you again before the weekend. Until then get plenty of rest, do whatever the doctors tell you, and most of all . . .

GET WELL SOON!

Your best friend forever,

Joyce

20

PEANUTS

« cartoon character

Do Your

⌃ nurse

⌃ gossip

Questions

_____ **1.** Why did Joyce write this card?

    a. To tell her friend about going to the beach.

    b. To tell her friend some jokes and gossip.

    c. To tell her friend she's worried about her.

    d. To tell her friend to be careful.

_____ **2.** What did Joyce do yesterday morning?

    a. She went to the hospital.   **b.** She went to the beach.

    c. She went to school.   **d.** She went to see a doctor.

_____ **3.** What is probably the reason why Kathy is in the hospital?

    a. She is very sick.   **b.** She wants to get gifts.

    c. She had an accident.   **d.** She's having a baby.

_____ **4.** What does "**this**" mean in the second paragraph?

    a. Kathy moving to another town.

    b. Joyce and Kathy having fun at school.

    c. Joyce's parents asking her about Kathy.

    d. Kathy getting hurt and going to the hospital.

_____ **5.** What does it mean when Joyce writes "**I'm running out of space**"?

    a. She's going to visit Kathy again.

    b. There's no more room to write on the card.

    c. She's exercising and can't write anymore.

    d. There's no place to put anything in her room.

» interview

7 Take Lemons and Make Lemonade

07

Host: We're here with former child star Jake Brannigan. You may remember Jake from the old television show *Who's in Charge*? He played the cute and mischievous David for five seasons. Now he's a waiter at a Chili's. Hello, Jake!

5 **Jake:** Oh, hello. And, not to **nitpick** or anything, but I'm actually an assistant manager.

Host: That's wonderful, Jake. Can you tell us about what it was like to work on *Who's in Charge*?

» lemonade

Questions

_____ 1. What is this reading about?
   a. A child actor.   **b.** A restaurant.
   c. A television show.   **d.** A film studio.

_____ 2. What does "**nitpick**" mean?
   a. To be all grown up.   **b.** To have a hard time choosing.
   c. To feel sorry for someone. **d.** To care too much about little details.

_____ 3. Which of the following statements about Jake Brannigan is not true?
   a. He played David on *Who's in Charge*?
   b. He was seven years old when he was on *Who's in Charge*?
   c. He runs a successful lemonade business.
   d. He did not manage his own money as a child.

Jake: It was a strange experience for a seven-year-old. Most kids that age are out on the playground, having fun with their friends. I was at the studio filming every day. It was kind of like having a full-time job at a very young age. I didn't even go to school.

Host: But you were **raking it in**, right? That must have been great for a little boy.

Jake: Not really. I was too young to manage the money I earned from *Who's in Charge?*

⌃ rake

Host: That's too bad! Well, how are you doing now? It must be a bit strange to go from star to server.

Jake: Actually, it's not so bad. When life gives you lemons, you just need to make lemonade.

Host: That's a very positive attitude. Good for you, Jake. Thanks for coming on the show, and we wish you all the best in your new career!

_____ 4. Which of the following is probably true?
  a. Jake never went to college.   **b.** *Who's in Charge?* is still on television.
  c. Jake hates working at Chili's.   **d.** Jake is too shy to be filmed.

_____ 5. What does "**raking it in**" mean?
  a. Serving a table.   **b.** Making a lot of money.
  c. Working full-time.   **d.** Being told what to do.

8 Take Me Out to the Ball Game

Major League Baseball (MLB) has been around since 1903, making it one of the oldest sports leagues in North America. Some might even say that MLB is "as American as apple pie." Many Americans have happy memories of **taking in** a game with their parents when they were young.

5 Tickets to go and see a ball game aren't always the same price. They tend to increase or decrease depending on which day of the week it is. The most expensive tickets are for games on Fridays and weekends. The cheapest games are in the middle of the week. The difference in prices can be pretty substantial. If you go to a game on Wednesday, you'll save 10 $23 on average compared to a Saturday game. For baseball fans, it really pays to have some free time during the week!

» The New York Yankees have won the most World Series Championships with 27.

Questions

_____ 1. What is this reading about?
- **a.** American landscapes.
- **b.** Sports.
- **c.** Ticket sales.
- **d.** Online games.

_____ 2. According to the bar chart, which is the most expensive day of the week to see a baseball game?
- **a.** Sunday.
- **b.** Saturday.
- **c.** Tuesday.
- **d.** Friday.

_____ 3. What does "**taking in**" a game mean?
- **a.** Watching it.
- **b.** Hearing about it.
- **c.** Selling a ticket for it.
- **d.** Giving up on it.

Daily Ticket Prices for Major League Baseball

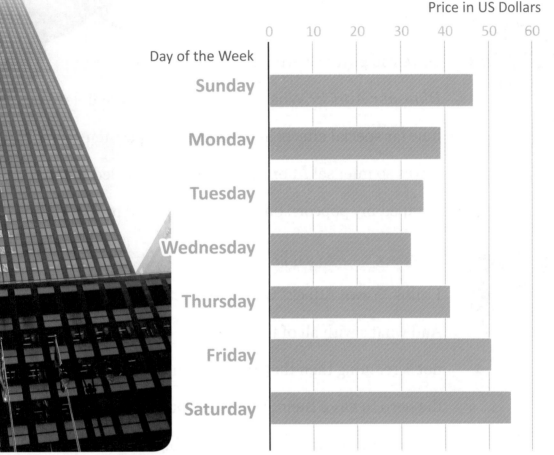

_____ **4.** What's the most likely reason that games during the week are cheaper than weekend games?

    a. Because the best players only play on the weekend.

    b. Because weekday games are twice as long.

    c. Because most people are busy during the week.

    d. Because better food is served for weekend games.

_____ **5.** According to the bar chart, which of the following is the cheapest day to see a baseball game?

    a. Friday.   **b.** Thursday.   **c.** Sunday.   **d.** Monday.

9 Everyone's a Movie Critic

« dinosaur

John

At 14:15, Posted by John

Have you guys seen that new movie called *Dinosaur Attack*? What a thrill ride! It's incredible how far special effects have come in the past ten years. It was so intense! At one point I was so startled that I dumped my popcorn on the person next to me.

5

Julie

At 14:15, Posted by Julie

I think "Yawn Attack" would be a better name for the movie. And what's with all of the women in the movie? If they're not screaming then they're hiding in a corner, waiting for the hero to **save** them. I think it would be nice to see some strong female **role models** on the big screen for once.

10

Bob

At 14:16, Posted by Bob

Everyone's a critic! It's just a movie, Julie. We watch them to forget about the world and have some fun. You shouldn't read so much into it. Just sit back and relax.

15

» dump

Julie

☐ At 14:20, Posted by **Julie**   20

Easy for you to say, Bob. You men aren't the ones screaming and crying in every single movie. You should ask yourself what we want to teach our young girls. Should they be strong and independent, or sweet little things who need to be saved by men?   25

What they see at the movies *does* make a difference.

Questions

____1. What is this reading about?

    a. Dinosaurs. **b.** Women.   **c.** A movie.   **d.** "Yawn Attack."

____2. Which of the following is not true?

    a. John loved *Dinosaur Attack*.   **b.** Bob thinks movies are for fun.

    c. Bob hated *Dinosaur Attack*.   **d.** Julie doesn't agree with Bob's post.

____3. What is a "role model"?

    a. Someone who's a good example for others to follow.

    b. Someone who makes money by posing for photographs.

    c. Someone who watches a lot of movies.

    d. Someone who's famous for acting in movies.

____4. Which of the following sounds like another movie John would like?

    a. *Wild Hearts.*   **b.** *Giant Robot Force.*

    c. *Dream of a Farmer.*   **d.** *A Cat's Life.*

____5. Which of the following sentences uses "save" in the same way as the reading?

    a. He took a shot, but it was saved by the goalkeeper.

    b. John saves half of every paycheck.

    c. Remember to save often when working on a computer.

    d. The little boy was saved by the fireman.

» parking lot

You Can't Park Here

To the owner of this motorcycle,

I have seen your vehicle parked here many times over the past few weeks. As you may or may not be aware, this is a private parking spot. It is illegal for you to park here.

5   I know it's tempting to take any empty spot, especially in an area like this. However, **try putting yourself in my shoes**. Sometimes I get home after an 11-hour shift and can't even park at my own home. That means I need to circle the block over and over, looking for a spot.

Illegal parking is a big problem for my building. Many of my
10 neighbors are not as kind as I am. They will skip the warning and **call** a tow truck right away. The unlucky person who gets towed then needs to pay to get his or her vehicle back. It can cost as much as 3,000 NTD. I prefer to warn the person first, and hope that he or she will do the right thing.

» vehicles

15   Please don't park your vehicle here again. And if you happen to see someone else doing the same thing, pass this message on. I am hoping that a positive approach works better than calling a tow truck.

20 Yours,

Jim

» tow truck

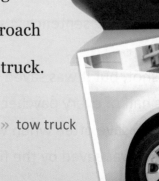

⌃ paying for parking at a pay station

Questions

_____ 1. What is this note about?

    a. A tow truck.   **b.** A parking spot.

    c. A motorcycle.   **d.** A city.

_____ 2. How is the writer different from his neighbors?

    a. He calls a tow truck right away.

    b. He doesn't have a parking spot.

    c. He always gives a warning first.

    d. He paid 3,000 NTD to get his vehicle back.

_____ 3. What does the writer mean when he says, "**try putting yourself in my shoes**" ?

    a. He is trying to be generous.

    b. He can't even buy a new pair of shoes.

    c. He doesn't let people walk on him.

    d. Try seeing things from his point of view.

_____ 4. Which of the following is probably true?

    a. It's very hard to find a parking spot where the writer lives.

    b. The writer drives a tow truck for a living.

    c. The writer rents his parking spot out to someone else.

    d. All of the writer's neighbors walk to work every day.

_____ 5. Which of the following sentences uses "**call**" in the same way as the reading?

    a. It took three hours for Tim to call me back.

    b. She heard Jim calling her from outside the house.

    c. They called their second dog Mortimer.

    d. He called heads and lost the coin toss.

11 | St. Patrick's Day Parade

The St. Patrick's Day parade has been a proud tradition of this town for over 50 years. It began as a way to honor the contributions of immigrants in building this country. Now it has become a key part of our community. It is an event that everyone looks forward to each year. When the snow begins to melt, we know that the St. Patrick's Day parade is just around the corner.

⌃ parade

⌃ float

Town Map

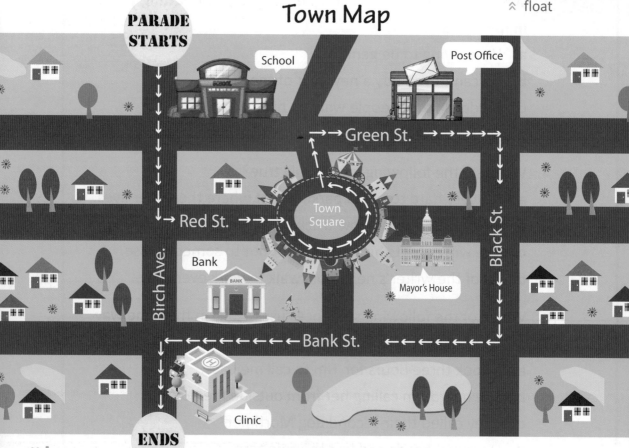

This year's parade will be **one for the history books**. For
10 the first time ever, citizens from other towns will be participating.
Each town will build its own float. On parade day, these floats
will move along the usual parade route. After that, everyone will
be able to vote for his or her favorite float. The winning town will
earn the title of "Float King"—at least until next year's parade.

» immigrants

Questions

_____ 1. What is this article about?
  a. A special event.   **b.** A town.
  c. A street.   **d.** A vote.

_____ 2. According to the map, where does the parade begin?
  a. Near Town Square.   **b.** Near the mayor's house.
  c. Near the bank.   **d.** Near the school.

_____ 3. What does it mean that this year's parade will be "one for
        the history books"?
  a. It will be based on the town's traditions.
  b. It will be remembered for years to come.
  c. It will be canceled.
  d. It will follow a different route.

_____ 4. According to the map, which of the following locations does
        the parade not pass by?
  a. The bank.   **b.** The school.
  c. The post office.   **d.** The mayor's house.

_____ 5. Where does the parade finish?
  a. Near the mayor's house. **b.** Near Town Square.
  c. Near the clinic.   **d.** Near the bank.

12 Courage

It could happen to you, on any given day.

It could happen to you, in any number of ways.

Because we all think we're good, and will stand up and figh

We all think that what's wrong will lose to what's right.

But we can't know for sure until put to the test. 5

And our final scores can be hard to digest.

Courage, a spirit that moves history with its force.

Courage, a spirit of which I can find no source.

My own test happened in the schoolyard last week.

Before which I would never have called myself meek. 10

But when I saw four guys bullying that kid.

There was no rescue from me; I **turned tail** *and hid.*

Now he has stopped coming to school.

His only crime was not being "cool."

Courage, how is it that you choose 15

Those who rise up, and those who refuse?

Days went by and the kid still didn't show.

I decided to ask around, see what people know.

The kid was a loner, almost like he had no friends.

No games or jokes; for himself he did fend. 20

Now he's gone and I fear never coming back.

If only I had done something, and got him on the right track.

Courage, you left me at such great cost.

Courage, you left me and now I am lost.

Questions

⌃ schoolyard

_____ 1. What is this poem trying to say?

    a. It's not always easy to do what's right.

    b. We all need to take tests at school.

    c. Bullying is becoming a big problem.

    d. Courage is a force that moves history.

⌃ bully

_____ 2. Why is the writer worried?

    a. He is being bullied at school.

    b. A bullied kid stopped coming to school.

    c. He is turning into a bully.

    d. He is good friends with a bully.

_____ 3. What does it mean that the writer "**turned tail**"?

    a. He stood up and fought the bullies.   **b.** He ran away.

    c. He tried talking to the bullies.   **d.** He didn't know what to do.

_____ 4. How does the writer probably feel about himself?

    a. He is happy.   **b.** He is excited.

    c. He is disappointed.   **d.** He is proud.

_____ 5. What happened in the schoolyard last week?

    a.   **b.**   **c.**   **d.**

13 Save Our Park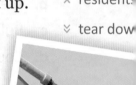

Calling All Residents of Glendale

It's time to **pull together** and save the park that we love. As many of you know, there has been a lot of talk about the city tearing down Shady Corners Park. The reasoning is that the park is already in bad shape. Some of those **bean counters** believe it would be cheaper to tear the park down than to fix it up.

However, there's more to it than that. Certain developers want the park to be torn down so that they can build new houses. They don't care about our children or our neighborhood; they just want to make some money! Some of these developers even have close connections with the city government.

Are the residents of Glendale going to sit back and let this happen? No! Everyone must get involved if we're to save Shady Corners. There are two important tasks that everyone must perform:

1. Come out for our park clean-a-thon on Saturday, May 10th. We're going to beautify the park ourselves so that the city does not have an excuse to tear it down.

2. Call your city representative. Let him or her know how you feel about the plan to redevelop Shady Corners. Together, we can make our elected officials change their minds!

residents

tear dow

« neighborhood

⌃ bean counter

Questions

_____ 1. What's the main idea of this reading?

   a. Developers are greedy people.

   b. People should care about their neighborhood.

   c. Shady Corners Park is in bad shape.

   d. It costs more to fix the park than to tear it down.

_____ 2. Why do the developers want the park to be torn down?

   a. To save money for the city government.

   b. To beautify the neighborhood.

   c. To put up new houses where the park was.

   d. To build a new park in its place.

_____ 3. What is a "**bean counter**"?

   a. Someone who plants beans for a living.

   b. Someone who only cares about saving money.

   c. Someone who is great at math.

   d. Someone who hates being outside.

_____ 4. Which of the following is probably true?

   a. The developers and the government are working together.

   b. The park is in bad shape because of the developers.

   c. The government doesn't have the money to tear the park down.

   d. The writer of this leaflet works for the government.

_____ 5. What does it mean to "**pull together**"?

   a. Move a heavy object.   **b.** Go backwards.

   c. Calm down.   **d.** Do a job as a group.

14 School Talent Show

» juggle

David: May, have you seen this poster?

May: Yeah, are you thinking about taking part?

David: Definitely! Didn't you know that I'm a **comedian**?

May: Oh, really?

5 David: Really.

May: All right. Tell me a joke, then.

David: Okay. Why didn't the skeleton go to the party?

May: I don't know. Why didn't the

10 skeleton go to the party?

David: Because he had *no body* to go with him.

May: . . .

David: **What**? That's funny!

15 May: Funny isn't really the word I'd use . . .

David: Okay, what about this one? What do you call a blind deer?

20 May: No idea.

David: Correct!

The Jamestown Junior H
Talent Show
Is Coming Soon . .

Can you . . .

☑ Play an Instrument? ☑ Juggle
☑ Do Magic? ☑ Sing?
☑ Tell Jokes? ☑ Dance?

To take part in the show, sign up with Miss O'Brian in the Drama department at breaktime. You must sign up by the end of this week!

First Prize: $100
Second Prize: $50
Third Prize: $20

May: What?

David: No-eye deer! Get it?

May: Well, I guess that was a little funny.

25 David: See, I told you I was a comedian. So, are you taking part, too?

May: I'd like to sing, but I don't think my voice is good enough.

David: You definitely should. You have an amazing voice!

May: Is that one of your lame jokes?

David: No, I'm serious. I think you could even win the whole thing!

Questions

_____ 1. What is the topic of David and May's conversation?
   a. Who they think will win the talent show.
   b. What they'll do with the prize money if they win.
   c. What they're going to do in the talent show.
   d. How to sign up for the talent show.

_____ 2. Why is May unsure about entering the show?
   a. She's feeling too sick to enter.
   b. She might be away on vacation.
   c. She has too much homework.
   d. She doesn't think she's good enough.

_____ 3. What is a "comedian"?
   a. Someone who sings.   b. Someone who makes people laugh.
   c. Someone who dances.   d. Someone who plays an instrument.

_____ 4. Who is most likely organizing the talent show?
   a. David.   b. One of the music teachers.
   c. May.   d. One of the drama teachers.

_____ 5. What does David mean when he asks, "What?"
   a. Why aren't you laughing?   b. What did you say?
   c. I don't get the joke.   d. I don't believe you.

15 The Street Store

To: jerrywang@freemail.com

Subject: The Street Store

Hi, Jerry!

How are things? I thought I'd tell you about something cool I saw on the street the other day. I was walking home from school when I saw a group of people gathered around these strange-looking posters. Each poster had a

5 picture of a clothes hanger on it, and at the bottom there was a slit which you could hang clothes through. But not new clothes. These were second-hand clothes for homeless people. It was a pop-up street market where you could take clothes you didn't want. Homeless people could then go there and "shop" for free clothes.

10 What a great idea, right? It's called the Street Store. I checked it out online. It started in South Africa, but **they**'re trying to spread the idea around the world. You can sign up on their website and get all the poster designs, information packs, etc. for free! Maybe you could start one in Taiwan?

Hope you're well!

15 Sally

» clothes hanger

Questions

_____ 1. What are Sally and Jerry discussing?
   a. Helping homeless people.   b. Buying second-hand clothes.
   c. Attending a family event.   d. Selling clothes at a street market

_____ 2. What does Sally suggest that Jerry do?
   a. Go and help out his cousin.   b. Start a pop-up street market.
   c. Give money to the homeless.   d. Design a poster.

To: sally.smith@popmail.com

Subject: RE: The Street Store

Hi, Sally!

Great to hear from you. That does sound like a great idea. In fact, my cousin does something similar in Taiwan already. He's part of a student group called Share5 that holds events for homeless people.

20 I was originally going to start volunteering with my cousin at Share5, but maybe I could start my own market using the info you gave me. Thanks for telling me about it. I'll let you know how it goes!

Jerry

_____ 3. Who are "they" in Sally's email?

    a. Jerry's cousin and his friends.   **b.** The people behind the Street Store.

    c. Homeless people in the area.   **d.** Taiwanese students.

_____ 4. Which of these could most likely be a logo for The Street Store?

a.   **b.**   **c.**   **d.**

Hi, Sally!

Just a quick message to let you know that I did what you suggested. We had our first event yesterday! Loads of people came and donated their old clothes. Some people even **donated** clothes that they'd bought new especially for the event! It was a real success!

Best,

Jerry

_____ 5. What does "**donated**" mean?

    a. Gave away.   **b.** Bought.   **c.** Stole.   **d.** Took home.

Some Timely Inspiration

Dear Joanne,

I am so excited that my hand is shaking as I write this postcard. I just finished the first day of the Global Youth Development Summit in London and you'll never guess who I

5   met. It was in the hall after the summit. I bumped into someone, and when I looked up it was none other than Huang Shi, my idol! We talked for a bit and then she invited me to dinner. Over the course of the evening I told her about myself and the work my organization does. She had heard about us. I was floored!

10   I think this chance meeting saved my career. As you know, I have been working as an intern for over four years now. My organization helps a lot of poor kids, and I love that part of my

Questions

_____ 1. What is this reading about?
- **a.** A lucky meeting.
- **b.** An organization.
- **c.** An intern.
- **d.** The Global Youth Development Sum

_____ 2. Which of the following is not true about Huang Shi?
- **a.** She is Kate's idol.
- **b.** She had trouble finding a job.
- **c.** She had dinner with Kate.
- **d.** She is Kate's boss.

_____ 3. What does it mean that Kate was "floored"?
- **a.** She was sad.
- **b.** She was shocked.
- **c.** She was confused.
- **d.** She was angry.

» intern

» bump into

job. However, I've been worried about my own future lately. Can I go on working as an underpaid intern for the rest of my life?

That's where Ms. Huang comes in. She told me about her 15 own struggles to find meaningful work right out of school. How crazy is that? Huang Shi, the legend, had problems finding work. She said I should keep fighting the good fight. She also said that a new position would be opening up in her organization in six months. I'm going to send my information directly to her! 20

I just had to tell someone. What an inspiration!

Love,

Kate

_____ 4. Which of the following is likely the name of Kate's organization?
   a. Save the Children.   **b.** Force for the Trees.
   c. Feed the World.   **d.** Teaching to Live Again.

_____ 5. Which of the following sentences uses "**course**" in the same way as the reading?
   a. It was his first time playing that golf course.
   b. The main course of the meal was steak.
   c. Her grades improved over the course of the school year.
   d. I'm taking a business course this semester.

17 Hi, I'm Tony. I'm Looking for . . .

Basic Information

Name: Tony Wang	Age: 16
English Ability: Excellent	
Mandarin Ability: Basic	
City: Taipei	Ad Posted: 12/07/2016
Looking For: Friendship/Language Exchange	

About Me

Hi, everyone. I'm Tony. I grew up in New York, but my family moved back to Taiwan a few weeks ago.

What I'm Looking For

My Chinese isn't great. I can speak a little, but I really need to practice wi
someone. Also, I don't really know anyone my age in Taipei. I was hoping
to find someone to hang out with who'd also be willing to help me with m
Chinese. In return, maybe I can help you with your English homework!

Hobbies/Interests

I like going to the movies (scary movies are my favorite), playing online games, and just hanging out.
like the food here a lot, but I don't really know any go
places to eat. Maybe you could introduce me to some

« scary movie

44

∧ night market

cool places to get snacks and drinks. I'd

like to start exploring some of the night

markets here, too. I'm also starting to get

really into photography, so I hope you

won't mind me stopping now and again to

take some **snaps**! I'm **not too keen on**

sports, and I'm not really into pop music.

So if you really love those things then we

probably won't have much to talk about!

Anything else?

Don't be shy! Send me a message!

∧ playing online games

Questions

_____ 1. What is Tony looking for?
- a. A new job.
- b. A lost friend.
- c. A roommate.
- d. A Chinese teacher.

_____ 2. Which of the following is Tony not interested in?
- a. Scary movies.
- b. Taking photographs.
- c. Popular music.
- d. Playing online games.

_____ 3. What are "**snaps**"?
- a. Photographs.
- b. Songs.
- c. Movies.
- d. Snacks.

_____ 4. Which of these can we guess about Tony?
- a. He can speak three languages.
- b. His parents are from Taiwan.
- c. He can't read or write English.
- d. He doesn't eat meat.

_____ 5. How do you feel about something that you're "**not too keen on**"?
- a. You love it.
- b. You're afraid of it.
- c. You don't like it very much.
- d. You would like to try it.

Hi, I'm Tony. I'm Looking for . . .

17

45

18 Graduation

» graduation ceremony

Tuesday, June 17

It's over! Today was the last day. Now I can finally congratulate myself for a job well done, years of hard work, and never giving up. These few years have been tough; that's for sure. I worked so hard

5 to get good grades so I could get into the best school, it almost drove me crazy! But it **all paid off in the end**. In September, I'll be going to my dream high school! And after that . . . who knows? I feel like the whole world is at my feet, like I could do anything!

Questions

_____ 1. What is the main subject of Jenny's diary entry?
   a. Her coming vacation to Thailand.
   b. Her feelings on finishing a stage in her life.
   c. Her least favorite subject at school.
   d. Her plans for the future.

_____ 2. Which of these did Jenny not do in the last few years?
   a. Work hard.   **b.** Make good friends.
   c. Give up.   **d.** Get good grades.

_____ 3. What is "It"?
   a. Junior high school.   **b.** High school.
   c. Her vacation.   **d.** June.

But the more I think about moving on, the sadder I get. I'll really miss the friends I made here, and the teachers who inspired and helped me. I'll miss Jane and her silly jokes, Eric with his goofy hairstyles, and Miss Zhou, who helped me so much with math.

But I guess there's plenty of time to remember later. Now it's time to celebrate! Goodbye textbooks, homework, and staying up late studying. Hello two weeks of fun in the sun! Dad told me after I came home that we're all going away to Thailand as a graduation surprise! I'm so relived to finally be able to take a break (though I wish my stupid brother didn't have to come too)!

That's all for now!

Jenny

10

15

20

» stay up late

⌃ textbook

4. Who is Eric?
   a. Jenny's father.
   b. Jenny's school friend.
   c. Jenny's math teacher.
   d. Jenny's brother.

5. What does it mean if something "all paid off in the end"?
   a. Terrible things happened because of it.
   b. The results were kept a secret.
   c. The results were unexpected.
   d. Good things resulted from it.

47

19 A Special Evening

John and Silvia celebrated their first anniversary by eating out at one of the city's most exclusive French restaurants. It was a lovely evening. Silvia was **dressed to the nines**, and John had an opportunity to order his favorite dessert. They had such a great time that they didn't even care about how expensive the meal was. Here i their order, and a poster advertising the restaurant.

» hamburger

≈ beef bourguig

GUEST CHECK

TABLE	PERSONS	989007	SERVER

Le Canard Gras

Table: **4**

Order taken: Bernard

Date: 07/26/2016

1	Beef bourguignon		1,000 TWD
1	Hamburger		800 TWD
1	Steamed mussels		600 TWD
1	Shrimp cocktail		600 TWD
1	Ice cream sundae		250 TWD
1	Bottle of French red wine		1,100 TWD
2	Espresso		300 TWD
	Total		4,650 TWD

» ice cream sundae

» bottle of wine

≈ steamed mussels

≈ shrimp cocktai

« espresso

Questions

1. What is this reading about?
   - **a.** A bill.
   - **b.** A dinner.
   - **c.** A poster.
   - **d.** A cheese-tasting event.

2. Which of the following is not something that John and Silvia ordered?
   - **a.** French cheese.
   - **b.** An ice cream sundae.
   - **c.** A hamburger.
   - **d.** Espresso.

3. What does it mean that Silvia was "dressed to the nines"?
   - **a.** She was dressed up.
   - **b.** She was wearing old clothes.
   - **c.** She was happy to be there.
   - **d.** She was wearing nine pieces of clothing.

4. Which of the following did John probably order?
   - **a.** The shrimp cocktail.
   - **b.** The beef bourguignon.
   - **c.** The hamburger.
   - **d.** The ice cream sundae.

5. According to the bill, John and Silvia ordered a bottle of French wine and two espressos. How much did they have to pay for these drinks?
   - **a.** 600 TWD
   - **b.** 1,100 TWD
   - **c.** 1,400 TWD
   - **d.** 2,000 TWD

20 Survival Camp

There's a show on TV at the moment that my friend Rob and I love watching. It's called *Can You Survive the Wild?* It's so much fun. Basically, each week two people get dropped into the wilderness and see if they can survive for 7 days

5   in the wild. It got me thinking. If I ever got stranded in the wilderness, I **wouldn't have a clue** how to survive! Rob said the same thing. So we've signed up for the Greenwood Teen Summer Survival Camp this summer. Here's the poster. We can't wait to learn lots of cool survival skills!

Questions

» walking boots

_____ 1. Which of these is the summer camp's main teaching focus?
- **a.** How to safely start a fire.
- **b.** How to survive in the wild.
- **c.** How to keep dry at night.
- **d.** How to hunt for small animals.

⌃ warm clothes

_____ 2. Which of the following is true?
- **a.** The writer will be attending the camp by himself.
- **b.** The writer will need to bring a sleeping bag to the camp.
- **c.** The writer's experience will be filmed for a TV show.
- **d.** There's a limit on how many people can attend each camp.

_____ 3. What does it mean if you "**don't have a clue**"?
- **a.** You don't know.
- **b.** You don't remember.
- **c.** You don't have time.
- **d.** You don't think it is right.

The Greenwood Teen Summer Survival Camp!

Join us and have a wild adventure! We teach you how to . . .

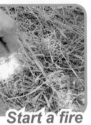
Start a fire

Trap small animals

Build a waterproof shelter

Find drinking water

Find your way without a compass using the sun and stars and lots more!

Camp Dates

Camp 1	Camp 2	Camp 3	Camp 4
2–13-year-olds only	14–15-year-olds only	16–17-year-olds only	18–19-year-olds only
July 10–17	July 20–27	August 2–8	August 12–18

What you'll need to bring:

•*Walking boots*   •*Warm clothes*   •*A positive attitude!*

There's only space for 20 people per camp, so sign up now!

_____ 4. The writer and his friend are 14 years old. Which camp are they attending?

    a. Camp 1.   **b.** Camp 2.   **c.** Camp 3.   **d.** Camp 4.

_____ 5. Which of these is a compass?

    a.   **b.**   **c.**   **d.**

21 My Boss's Busy Schedule

Hi Michelle,

You asked me to email you your calendar for next month, so here **it** is. I'm afraid it's going to be a busy one!

5 If you want me to move or change any of your **appointments**, just let me know. By the way, your tickets for London are on your desk. And your husband called; he asked if you could

10 call him back before 5 o'clock.

Thanks,

Anita

Mon	Tue
6 Meeting with senior managers about the fall collection (11:00)	**7** Video cal to Shangl office (08
13	**14**
20 Breakfast meeting at the Adore Store (07:30)	**21**
27	**28** Video call New York office (13:

Questions

_____ 1. What is an "appointment"?
   a. A meeting at an agreed time.
   b. A meeting in the evening.
   c. A meeting of more than ten people.
   d. A meeting that happens by video.

_____ 2. Which sentence is true about Michelle?
   a. She works in London every Thursday.
   b. She is married.
   c. She never starts work before 8 a.m.
   d. She is Anita's secretary.

Wed	Thu	Fri	Sat	Sun
	2 All day at London office (train 07:20)	**3** Meeting at Perfect Perfumes (10:30)	**4** Lunch with Jack and Leonie, Rabbit Café (12:00)	**5**
8 Presentation to Fashion Plus (15:00)	**9**	**10**	11	
15	**16** All day at London office (train 07:20)	**17**		**19** Edward's birthday party (19:00)
22 Sales conference in Liverpool (train 06:35)	**23**	**24** Dinner with Clare, the Willows (20:00)	**25**	**26** ⩒ swimwear
29 Presentation on swimwear range (14:00)	**30** All day at London office (train 07:20)			

_____ 3. What does the reading tell us about?

    a. Someone's mistake.   **b.** Someone's problems.

    c. Someone's good idea.   **d.** Someone's plans.

_____ 4. Which sentence describes Michelle and Anita's jobs?

    a. They design furniture.   **b.** They work in fashion.

    c. They own a café.   **d.** They sell vacations.

_____ 5. What does "it" mean here?

    a. A month.   **b.** An email.   **c.** A calendar.   **d.** A ticket.

53

22 Recipe of the Week: Panda Bear Cookies

Kids will love to make these cute cookies! They're quick, easy, and great for parties. Be sure to help your children with sharp knives and hot ovens. 5

You will need:

1. 300 grams flour

5. 10 grams orange skin

2. 225 grams butter

6. an egg

3. 110 grams sugar

7. a **pinch** of salt

4. 10 grams cocoa powder

How to make the cookies:

1. Switch on your oven to 350 degrees.

2. Put the butter and sugar in a 10 bowl. Stir them together with a spoon.

3. Add the egg and orange skin.

4. Mix in the salt and flour, little by little, using your fingers. 15

Questions

_____ 1. How long should you leave the dough in the fridge?
   a. Ten minutes.
   b. Half an hour.
   c. One hour.
   d. Two hours.

_____ 2. What does "**it**" mean here?
   a. The dough.
   b. Cocoa powder.
   c. An hour.
   d. The fridge.

5. You should now have cookie dough. Cut the dough in half with a knife.

6. Add cocoa powder to one half of the dough, to make **it** brown. Put it in the fridge for an hour.

7. Cover your kitchen surface with flour. Take the other half of your dough and roll it flat. Cut it into panda-shaped cookies.

8. Take the brown dough out of the fridge. Cut shapes for the pandas' eyes, ears, arms and legs.

9. Bake the cookies for 10-12 minutes.

10. Leave the cookies to cool down, and then keep them in a closed box.

Enjoy!

3. Which sentence is true?
   a. You should mix the salt and flour in very quickly.
   b. Straight after baking, put the cookies in a box.
   c. You need more sugar than butter for these cookies.
   d. Children need adults' help to make these cookies.

4. What is a "**pinch**"?
   a. A small amount.   b. A large plate.
   c. A kind of food.   d. A place to cook.

5. What does the passage tell us?
   a. How to cook different meats.
   b. How to take care of animals.
   c. How to make something sweet.
   d. How to stay safe in the kitchen.

23 New Planet Discovered

⌄ NASA logo

Scientists have discovered a new planet that is similar to Earth. The planet, called Kepler-186f, is slightly (no more than 10%) larger than **ours** and probably has seasons like Earth does. But while this news is exciting, there is a lot that we still don't know about Kepler-186f.

NASA – the research organization that found the new planet – is always looking for planets with similar **conditions** to Earth's. However, space scientist Thomas Barclay says that we should think of Kepler-186f as an **"Earth cousin"** and not as an "Earth twin." Like our planet, it is made of rock. It is also likely to have water on its surface, which is unusual, but in many other ways Kepler-186f is different from Earth.

Whereas Earth takes 365 days to go around the sun, Kepler-186f only takes 130 days to go around its star. Earth is brighter, too; at midday on Kepler-186f, the sky would look the same as during our sunset. And scientists don't yet know about the temperature on the new planet. There is a good chance that Kepler-186f is much hotter than Earth.

Unfortunately, humans will not be traveling to Kepler-186f any time soon. It is 500 light-years away, so the journey would take a lot more than 500 years. NASA is still looking for other livable planets which are closer and easier to understand.

⌃ comparison of best-fit size of Kepler-186f with Earth
(cc by Aldaron)

« artist's concept of Kepler-186f   ⌄ solar system

Pluto
Uranus
Neptune
Mars
Venus
Jupiter
Earth
Mercury
Saturn

Questions

1. Which is the best picture to go with the passage?

a.   b.   c.   d.

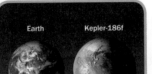

2. Which sentence is true about Kepler-186f?

   a. It has seasons.   **b.** It is 365 years old.

   c. It has mountains.   **d.** It is quite cold.

3. What does "**ours**" mean?

   a. Our feelings.   **b.** Our lives.

   c. Our families.   **d.** Our planet.

4. Why does Thomas Barclay say that Kepler-186f is an "**Earth cousin**"?

   a. There is ice on it.   **b.** Nobody lives on it.

   c. It is similar to Earth.   **d.** It is hotter than Earth.

5. What does "**conditions**" mean in the reading?

   a. Skills.   **b.** Scientists.   **c.** Weight.   **d.** Environment.

Mark's Moving Sale Blowout

I've learned a lot over the past four years, but it's time to move on and start my career. Lucky for you there are all these great items I can't bring with me. So come one, come all. Everything must go!

Where: 25 Bluebird Drive
When: Saturday, August 5, 2:00 p.m.

What's **Up for Grabs**:

1. Keal Dresser 15,000 TWD

This dresser is one of the high-end models that Keal offers. It's great for storing your clothes in style. It might already be four years old, but I think it will last a lifetime. I'm sorry I can't bring this one with me.

Questions

____ 1. Which of the following is not true?
   a. Mark is selling a dresser from Keal.
   b. Mark is selling a table and chairs.
   c. Mark likes playing video games.
   d. Mark painted his own wooden table.

____ 2. What is a "blowout"?
   a. A dangerous item that you should stay away from.
   b. A party where everyone plays video games.
   c. An event where things are sold very cheaply.
   d. A gathering where second-hand items are collected for poor people

2. PlayStation 4 10,000 TWD

This PlayStation has served me well, but I need the money and will have less time for video games now. Two games and an extra controller are included.

3. Wooden Table 6,000 TWD

This one is a real treasure. It wasn't bought at any store; I found it at an estate sale. I took it home, restored it, and painted it. Now it looks as good as new. My loss is your gain here.

4. Television Stand 900 TWD

What is there to say about a television stand? I guess this one is pretty handy because it helps you hide the cords from your electronics.

____3. Which of the following is probably true about Mark?
- **a.** He just got offered a new job in another city.
- **b.** He doesn't own a television.
- **c.** He doesn't need to worry about money.
- **d.** He hates working with his hands.

____4. What is this reading about?
- **a.** A supermarket.　**b.** A sale.　**c.** A dresser.　**d.** A party.

____5. What does it mean if something is "**up for grabs**"?
- **a.** It's popular.　**b.** It's old.　**c.** It's expensive.　**d.** It's available.

25 Living Murphy's Law

25

You woke up 20 minutes late this morning. Racing through breakfast, you spilled black tea on your school uniform. Your mother saw this and got angry at you. The beautiful weather turned to rain while you were on your way to school—without an umbrella. When you arrived, your teacher

5 announced a surprise quiz in math, your worst subject.

Sound familiar? If so, you may be **living Murphy's law**: Whatever *can* go wrong, *will* go wrong.

Chances are you've heard some version of Murphy's law somewhere. You may even have applied it to your own life at a time when nothing

10 seemed to go right. Or you may have applied it to someone else's life. Do you have a friend who always gets terrible marks, can't play any sport, and looks funny with any haircut? If so, you've probably thought or said, "If there's any way to do it wrong, he or she will." Call this Murphy's law in the third person.

15 But the law isn't always negative. An early version states that "Whatever can happen will happen," which sounds pretty optimistic if you're feeling good. And "Anything that can go wrong probably will" is a useful reminder to think of all possibilities before starting a task. Of course, it's also a **handy** excuse if you mess up that task!

20 Just where Murphy's law comes from is a mystery, but there's nothing mysterious about a bad day. Especially when you know how to describe it.

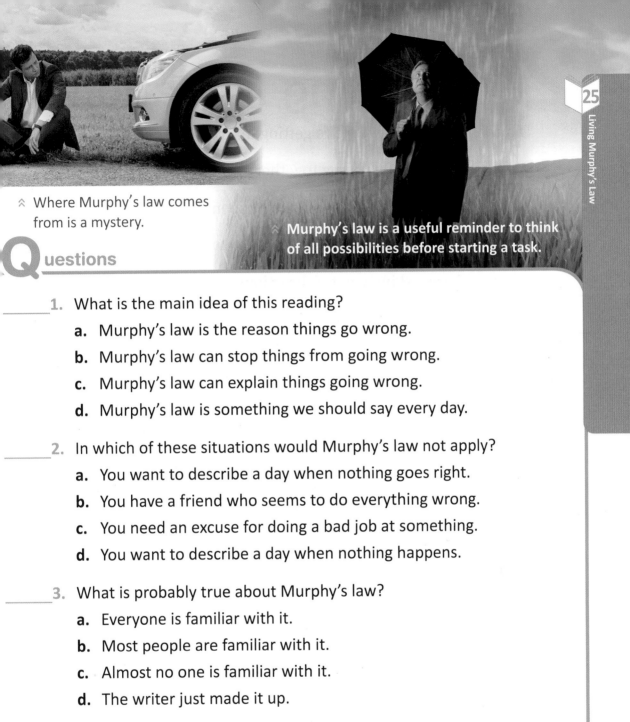

⌃ Where Murphy's law comes from is a mystery.

⌃ Murphy's law is a useful reminder to think of all possibilities before starting a task.

Questions

_____ 1. What is the main idea of this reading?

   a. Murphy's law is the reason things go wrong.

   b. Murphy's law can stop things from going wrong.

   c. Murphy's law can explain things going wrong.

   d. Murphy's law is something we should say every day.

_____ 2. In which of these situations would Murphy's law not apply?

   a. You want to describe a day when nothing goes right.

   b. You have a friend who seems to do everything wrong.

   c. You need an excuse for doing a bad job at something.

   d. You want to describe a day when nothing happens.

_____ 3. What is probably true about Murphy's law?

   a. Everyone is familiar with it.

   b. Most people are familiar with it.

   c. Almost no one is familiar with it.

   d. The writer just made it up.

_____ 4. What does "handy" mean?

   a. Negative.   **b.** Positive.   **c.** Useful.   **d.** Mysterious.

_____ 5. Which of these people is "living Murphy's law"?

   a.   **b.**   **c.**   **d.**

Dianne: I can't believe we're getting married after all this time. I mean, after being together ten years you start to assume it's never going to happen. Yet here we are . . .

Paul: Has it really been ten years? Wow, it seems like just yesterday I was asking you for directions to the campus library.

Dianne: Directions that you didn't even need, you little con artist. You knew exactly where the library was; you were studying there three times a week!

Paul: Well, it worked, didn't it?

Dianne: I guess I got what I deserved for being tricked so easily.

Paul: How is the invitation coming along?

Dianne: It's almost done. Here, have a look.

Paul Smith
and
Dianne Jackson

You are invited to join Paul and Dianne as they finally *tie the knot*.

Where: St. Andrew's Church

When: 3:00 p.m. on May 25th, 2016.

What to bring: Yourself and a **plus-one**. After the church service we will walk as a group to a nearby restaurant for dinner and speeches. Afterwards there will be karaoke and dancing until the break of dawn There's only one thing you must do: please RSVP and let us know if you will be attending. If not, you'd better have a good excuse!

Reply Card

Please Respond by March 31st.

My name is _____.

Yes! Of course I'll be there _____, and
I'm bringing a plus-one: _____.

No! But I have a good excuse: _____.

⌃ wedding

Questions

1. What is this reading about?

   a. An artist.
   b. A library.
   c. A trick.
   d. A special day.

2. According to the card, what happens after the church service?

   a. The guests go home.
   b. The guests sing karaoke.
   c. The guests eat dinner.
   d. The guests give gifts.

3. What is a "**plus-one**"?

   a. Someone who is getting married.
   b. Someone whom an invited guest brings to a wedding.
   c. Someone who is a really good friend.
   d. Someone who goes to church every Sunday.

4. Where did Paul and Dianne probably first meet?

   a. At work.
   b. At school.
   c. At a family dinner.
   d. At a church.

5. What does it mean to "**tie the knot**"?

   a. To get married.
   b. To get a job.
   c. To throw a party.
   d. To fall in love.

27 | Tips for Learning English

It's not surprising that a lot of people are choosing to learn English. As the second-most-spoken language in the world, English can **open a lot of doors**. There's also the cultural draw of Hollywood and popular music.

The rise of English means there are lots of books to help English

5   learners. This is not always a good thing, though. Lots of different systems means lots of different rules, and when you put them all together it can get confusing. Luckily there are a few simple tips that apply to all English learners. They are as follows:

1. Don't be afraid to use your English. It may not be perfect yet, but you

10   should use it and let yourself make mistakes. That is how you'll learn.

2. Use different tools. There's a whole world of English books, movies, music, podcasts, and newspapers out there. Don't make the mistake of thinking your textbook is the **be-all and end-all** of learning English. You could even try making friends with native English-speakers on the

15   Internet to work on your skills.

3. Don't only focus on grammar textbooks. Sometimes the best way to learn grammar is to just listen to English-speakers. Don't worry too much about memorizing your grammar textbook.

4. Don't give up. English is known for being difficult to read and

20   having a huge vocabulary. Accept these challenges head-on,

     and don't even think of putting that English book down.

» Use different tools.

Questions

Don't be afraid to use your English.

_____1. What is this reading trying to say?

   a. English is a hard language to learn.

   b. English is one of the most popular languages.

   c. There are ways to learn English more effectively.

   d. There are lots of English learners in the world.

_____2. Which of the following is not a tip from the reading?

   a. Listen to English podcasts while you sleep.

   b. Don't worry about grammar textbooks.

   c. Try using different English materials.

   d. Believe in yourself and keep up the good work.

Don't only focus on grammar textbooks.

_____3. What does it mean that English can "**open a lot of doors**"?

   a. It teaches people about doors.

   b. It can help you succeed in life.

   c. It can help you live longer.

   d. It is spoken by more and more people.

_____4. Which of the following could be another tip in this reading?

   a. Study the history of world languages.

   b. Eat at least two types of vegetables each day.

   c. Jog twice a week to keep your mind in shape.

   d. Try keeping a diary to practice your writing skills.

_____5. What does it mean if something is the "**be-all and end-all**"?

   a. It has been lost forever.

   b. It is the most important thing.

   c. It is hard to understand.

   d. It will help you make new friends.

28 A Message for the Future

» capsule

Dear Citizen of the Future,

I am putting this note in a time capsule in the year 2016. It is to be opened in 2066.

All of the things we thought were high-tech, like smartphones
5 and GPS, are probably old-fashioned by now. You probably have robots and mind-control technology to play around with. I don't think robots will have taken over yet by 2066. But if so and it's a robot digging up my time capsule, please be nice to the humans; we're not all bad.

10 Jokes aside, I have a message for all the citizens of the future. You need to take better care of your planet. I am worried that you will resent people from my time for what we did to Earth. Ours

Questions

_____ 1. What is the writer trying to say in this note?
   a. Global warming is a big problem.
   b. Robots will be invented soon.
   c. One person can make a difference.
   d. People shouldn't work at banks.

_____ 2. How many years will it be until the writer's note is read by someone
   a. 50   **b.** 25   **c.** 30   **d.** 100

_____ 3. What does a time capsule possibly look like?
   a. A box.   **b.** A tree.   **c.** A shelf.   **d.** A sheet of paper.

was a wasteful society; that's for sure. There are many problems in 2016, like global warming, dirty oceans, and animals becoming extinct all over the world. **I can only imagine** that these problems will be even worse by 2066.

This brings me to my promise. I have decided to live my life for our planet. I quit my job at the bank and got a new job where I can make a real difference. I feel I did my part to help make 2066 a better year. Now I hope that you can do the same, stranger. We are only individuals, but if we all come together and do what's right, we can change the world.

⌄ sign marking the spot where a time capsule has been buried in Venice

TIME CAPSULE
BURIED
December 29, 1999
TO BE OPENED
2100

» time capsule in Emirates Stadium

TIME CAPSULE PLACED ON 28TH OCTOBER 2004

_____4. What does the writer mean by "**I can only imagine**"?
  a. The writer is sad about something.
  b. The writer is guessing.
  c. The writer doesn't know.
  d. The writer doesn't believe something.

_____5. Which of the following is likely the writer's new job?
  a. Traffic police officer.   **b.** Salesperson at a clothing store.
  c. Environmental journalist.   **d.** Artist.

29 Just Ask Lina

I updated my smartphone yesterday and discovered a neat new tool. It's called "Ask Lina." You just press this button here and then ask a question. It's totally nuts how smart Lina is. This isn't one of those old computer programs that faked artificial intelligence; Lina is the real deal.

Here, just check this out.

Question 1: What's the weather going to be like tomorrow?

Answer: It will be a sunny 30 degrees Celsius with a chance of thundershowers in the afternoon.

Question 2: What should I wear on my first day of school next week?

Answer: Tight jeans and polo shirts are very **hot** right now. However, judging from your Internet search history, you might feel more comfortable in a purple V-neck sweater and slacks.

Question 3: Wait. You can see my Internet search history?

Answer: Of course I can. Your phone company can see it, too. We know everything about you.

» artificial intelligence

⌄ V-neck sweater

⌃ slacks

What can I help you with?

Question 4: Is it legal to look at my search history without asking me?

Answer: You agreed to it the first time you turned your phone on.
             It's all in the buyer's contract; check page 84.

25 Question 5: That's Okay, I guess. Well, if you know everything about
               me, I may as well ask. Am I ever going to find a girlfriend?

Answer: Don't count on it.

Questions

1. What surprised the writer?
   a. Lina knew what the weather was going to be like tomorrow.
   b. Lina could pick the right clothes to wear.
   c. Lina knew the writer's Internet search history.
   d. Lina said the writer wasn't going to find a girlfriend.

2. What is this article about?
   a. A girl.   b. A tool.   c. A contract.   d. A computer.

3. What does it mean if something is "hot" right now?
   a. It's expensive.   b. It's popular.
   c. It's colorful.   d. It's used in winter.

4. Which of the following is probably true about the writer?
   a. The writer has a full-time job.
   b. The writer's favorite color is purple.
   c. The writer read the whole buyer's contract.
   d. The writer is married.

5. What is the weather going to be like tomorrow?
   a.   b.   c.   d.

30 | Our Planet Is Heating Up

» global warming

Global warming is one of the biggest problems of our time. The phrase refers to the slow, year-by-year increase in temperatures around the world. Most scientists believe that rising temperatures are

5 being caused by too much carbon dioxide (CO_2) in the atmosphere. Carbon dioxide is released when we burn fossil fuels. However, there are still a few scientists who believe that global warming is a natural trend. This group has made it difficult to

10 reach an agreement and **turn back the clock** on rising temperatures.

While people might not agree on the causes, they do agree on the effects of global warming. Rising temperatures result in less food being

15 grown, higher sea levels, and dangerous weather. Some say that global warming is already causing wars over smaller water and food supplies.

The good news is, we can all do our part. How much fossil fuel do you burn in your daily

20 life? Try to come up with ways to make your footprint smaller and help fix our planet.

» fossil fuels

» carbon dioxide (CO_2)

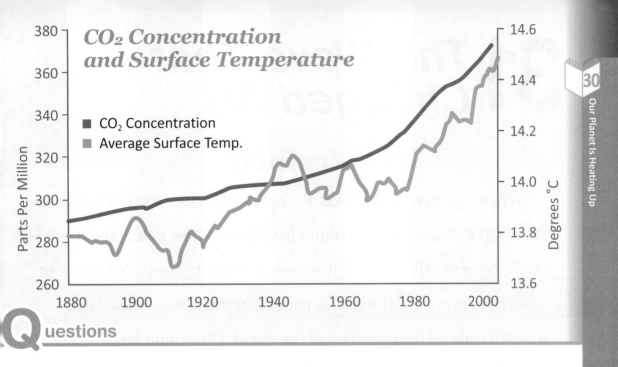

CO₂ Concentration and Surface Temperature

- CO₂ Concentration
- Average Surface Temp.

Questions

_____ 1. What is the main idea of this reading?

    a. Carbon dioxide is released when we burn fossil fuels.

    b. Global warming is a problem, but together we can beat it.

    c. Scientists don't agree on the causes of global warming.

    d. It's up to all of us to protect the planet.

_____ 2. According to the graph, what was the average surface temperature in 1900?

    a. 13.7   **b.** 14.2   **c.** 13.9   **d.** 14.4

_____ 3. What does it mean to "**turn back the clock**" on rising temperatures?

    a. Increase them.   **b.** Make them the way they were before.

    c. Beat them.   **d.** Make them stay the same.

_____ 4. What's most likely another effect of global warming?

    a. Animals living longer.   **b.** Less ice at the North Pole.

    c. Fewer earthquakes.   **d.** Healthier people.

_____ 5. According to the graph, what is true about the year 1910?

    a. It had colder winters than 2000.

    b. It had longer days than 1950.

    c. It had more CO₂ in the air than 1960.

    d. It had warmer summers than 1980.

Preface

When Japanese printmaker Katsushika Hokusai made *The Great Wave Off Kanagawa*, he couldn't have known how influential it would become. After all, the print was just one in a set of 36 different views of Mount Fuji. It was also painted in the 1820s, when Japan was still isolated from the rest of the world. How could he have known that it would have such a big impact so far from his island's shores?

⌃ *The Great Wave Off Kanagawa,* 1830–33

After Japan opened up in the 1850s, *The Great Wave* started **making waves** in the art world. Here is one of the greatest stories in the history of art. A Japanese printmaking technique influences the West, giving birth to a new art style. Then Western art comes back to influence Japan years later, when Art Deco sweeps the islands. The moral of this story is that art doesn't care about national borders; it's for all of us.

That *The Great Wave* influenced Western art and helped give birth to Impressionism is a fact. The open question, and one that this book wants to answer, is, *how big* was this impact? We know that great artists like Claude Monet loved Hokusai's prints, but how did

5

10

15

20

≫ *Madame Monet in a Japanese Kimono*, Monet, 1875

this love influence their work? This book **gets to the bottom** of things by examining each one of Monet's paintings. It compares the techniques used by Monet to those used by Hokusai. This careful examination tells us the true story of "the wave that changed art."

Questions

≫ Claude Monet

_____ 1. What is this article trying to say?

    a. Japanese art was more advanced than Western art.

    b. A Japanese artist had a big influence on Western art.

    c. Japan used to be isolated from the rest of the world.

    d. Japanese printmaking techniques were very unique.

_____ 2. What Western art movement became popular in Japan?

    a. Impressionism.   **b.** Japanese printmaking.

    c. Art Deco.   **d.** Claude Monet.

_____ 3. What does it mean that *The Great Wave* started "**making waves**" in the art world?

    a. It started changing things.   **b.** It was ignored.

    c. It was laughed at.   **d.** It started making art less popular.

_____ 4. Which of the following is likely a chapter from this book?

    a. The life story of Katsushika Hokusai.

    b. A brief history of Japanese art.

    c. The great masters of the Art Deco movement.

    d. *Women in the Garden*, by Claude Monet.

_____ 5. What does it mean to "**get to the bottom**" of something?

    a. To give something to it.   **b.** To discover the truth about it.

    c. To keep it away from you.   **d.** To improve it.

32 | Head Transplants

» perform an operation

Young Scientist Magazine
Old Head, New Body?

This month a doctor from Italy claimed he would soon be ready to perform the first-ever human head transplant.

5 As this is a new operation, there are lots of questions about head transplants. We answer some of them here.

Q: What is a head transplant?

A: A head transplant is where the head from one person is attached to the body of **another**.

10 Q: Where would the bodies come from?

A: The planned operation will use the body of a brain-dead donor. However, in the future it may be possible to grow headless bodies in a lab.

⌃ transplantation of a dog's head in Gemany
(cc by Weiß, Günter)

Q: Who would benefit from such an operation?

15 A: People whose brains are healthy but whose bodies are damaged beyond repair.

Q: Will the head be able to control the new body?

A: Doctors aren't sure yet. Plans are to use a special chemical that promot spine growth, but whether this will be enough is still not known.

20 Q: Is a head transplant the same as a brain transplant?

A: No. A brain transplant is where just the brain is moved from one body

⌃ repair

to another. In fact, this is much harder to perform than a head transplant, as damaging a brain is much more likely.

Q: What are the chances that the operation will succeed?

25 A: The doctor who will perform the surgery estimates his chances of success at 90%. Many other experts are, however, very doubtful. **Only time will tell.**

Questions

_____1. What does this article do?
   a. Give advice on how to stay healthy.
   b. Give advice on how to train your brain.
   c. Answer questions about a new operation.
   d. Answer questions about life as a doctor.

_____2. Which of these is true about the proposed operation?
   a. The doctor has performed the same operation many times.
   b. The body used will be a robotic one.
   c. The head may not be able to control the new body.
   d. The doctor in charge thinks the chance of success is low.

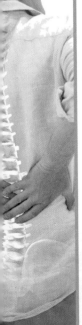
⌄ spine

_____3. What does "**another**" mean?
   a. Another person.   **b.** Another body.
   c. Another head.   **d.** Another doctor.

_____4. Which of these people might be a suitable subject for a head transplant?
   a. Someone with serious brain damage.
   b. Someone with damage to many of his or her organs.
   c. Someone who has trouble controlling his or her emotions.
   d. Someone who is addicted to drugs.

_____5. What is another way to say, "**Only time will tell**"?
   a. We need to know the answer right now.
   b. It's not a good time to talk about it.
   c. It's time we made a decision.
   d. We'll just have to wait and see.

» the logo of the Ministry
of Education of Finland

Ministry of Education and Culture

33 Schools in Finland: The Secret of Their Success

Finland's schools are the best in Europe, some might say in the world. Only three countries—China, Singapore, and South Korea—can compete with Finland in exam results. So, what is the secret of Finland's success?

Surprisingly, Finnish children spend less time in school than children

5 in many other countries. They don't start school until the age of seven, their school days are short, and their vacations are long. Education in Finland is relaxed. Classrooms often look like living rooms. Students don't wear uniforms and they call teachers by their first names. **What's more**, they have only 30 minutes of homework each night.

Questions

_____ 1. What is the passage about?
a. The everyday life of a teacher in a Finnish school.
b. The difference between Asian and European schools.
c. The subjects that are taught in American schools.
d. The reasons why Finnish schools get good results.

_____ 2. Which picture is most like a classroom in Finland?

a.    b.    c.    d.

University of Vaasa in Finland

Finnish flag

10   Many people believe that the Finnish system works because its teachers are so good. It's a popular, well-paid job, and teachers are usually kind and not strict. They also have an unusual way of teaching. Rather than having separate subjects like history and geography, 15 students learn everything together. There are seven things that Finnish students must learn in school:

- how to think clearly;
- how to understand and join in Finnish culture;
- how to use language, numbers and other information;
20 • how to use technology;
- how to take care of themselves;
- how to be successful at work; and
- how to be a good person for the future of Finland.

After finishing high school, Finnish students can also attend university for free. This is very different 25 from the United States, **where** the cost of a degree is around $30,000!

_____ 3. What does "**What's more**" mean?

   a. Also.   **b.** But.   **c.** Except.   **d.** Because.

_____ 4. Which statement is true?

   a. Not many Finnish people want to be teachers.
   b. A degree is cheaper in the United States than in Finland.
   c. Students in Singapore get very good exam scores.
   d. Korean teachers only have three weeks' vacation.

_____ 5. What does "**where**" mean?

   a. In high school.   **b.** In college.
   c. In the United States.   **d.** In Europe.

34 | How to Do Sit-Ups (34)

Do you wish you could turn your **flabby** belly into a rock-hard six-pack? It's certainly possible. By doing one simple exercise, you can turn that belly fat into solid muscle! I'm talking, of course, about sit-ups!

5　　There are a few different ways to perform sit-ups, some harder than others, but the classic sit-up is very easy to do. Here's how:

Step 1　Lie on your back and bend your knees so that your feet are flat on the floor.

10 Step 2　Place your hands behind your head.

Step 3　Now simply sit up! Keeping your feet flat, tighten your stomach muscles, lift your head first, then your shoulders, and keep going until your upper body is at a 90-degree angle to the floor.

Step 4　Wait! Don't drop back down right away. Hold that position for a second.

Step 5　Now, slowly drop your upper body back to the floor, keeping your shoulders just slightly elevated off the ground. This will help maintain the tension in your muscles, making your workout more effective.

biceps　delt・

triceps

belly

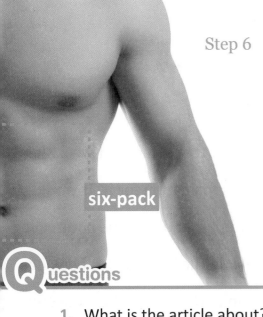

six-pack

Step 6　Repeat **this** as many times as you can. It doesn't matter if you can't do many on your first try. Just keep practicing, and try to increase the number of sit- ups you do each time. Soon you'll be saying goodbye to that belly fat and hello to a hard, flat stomach!

25

 Questions

_____1. What is the article about?
  a. A health problem.　　　　**b.** A new diet.
  c. A team sport.　　　　　　**d.** A type of exercise.

_____2. Which of these is true about classic sit-ups?
  a. You can do them standing up.
  b. They're difficult to do.
  c. They develop your stomach muscles.
  d. They require a helper.

_____3. What does the word "**flabby**" most likely mean?
  a. Flat.　　　**b.** Fatty.　　　**c.** Perfect.　　　**d.** Painful.

_____4. Which of these people is performing a sit-up?
  a. 　　　**b.**

  c. 　　　**d.**

_____5. What does "**this**" mean?
  a. Step 6.　　**b.** Steps 3 to 5.　**c.** Steps 2 to 4.　**d.** Step 3.

35 A Brief History of Canada  ⟨35⟩

I have a big history paper on Canada that's due next week. It has been a little difficult to find good information for it. It would have been impossible to write if I hadn't found this one book called *A Brief History of Canada*. The index in the back of that book has

5   been a **lifesaver**. It allows me to skip to the information I need without wasting any time. Now I can get to work writing that paper about the Europeans' earliest contact with aborigines in Canada.

Questions

1. What is this reading about?
   a. War.   **b.** Homework.   **c.** Canada.   **d.** Aborigines.

2. Which page should I look at if I want to learn more about the Durham Report?
   a. 75   **b.** 80   **c.** 120   **d.** 125

3. What is a "lifesaver"?
   a. Something that is hard to find.
   b. Something that you can't understand.
   c. Something that makes you proud.
   d. Something that helps you a lot.

INDEX

A

Aborigines   5-20, 25, 73
   Beliefs   5
   Contact with Europeans   7, 12
   Culture   5
   Tools   6
   Tribes   18
American Revolution   100-102

B

Borden, Robert   75-79, 81-85, 90
   Early Life   75
   First Term   78
   Policies   79
   Second Term   82
British Rule   50-125
   Early Stages   50-53
   End   124-125
   Government   55, 60, 62
   Laws   52
   War of 1812   105
   World War I   120-125

C

Canada Act   130
Chipewyan (Tribe)   18
Columbus, Christopher   26
Cowichan (Tribe)   18

D

Depression Years   150-223
   Policies   155
   Trade Effects   160
   World War II   170-199, 201, 204
Durham Report   80-85
   Causes   80
   Effects   84

≪ aborigines
≪ European

_____ 4. *"He was a two-term prime minister who changed Canada forever. He came into office with a view on what makes good policy, and that view never changed."* On what page would you find these sentences?

   a. 79   **b.** 130   **c.** 105   **d.** 20

_____ 5. Which of the following is probably true?

   a. There is only one tribe of aborigines in Canada.

   b. Canadian aborigines never made contact with Europeans.

   c. British rule ended after World War I.

   d. Canada did not fight in World War II.

36 | Soak Up Some Japanese Culture

Hot springs, or *onsens*, are an important part of Japanese culture. They come in all shapes and sizes, and are found all over Japan. They can be indoors, outdoors, public, or private. Some are found in cities, others in the countryside. However, they all share the same relaxing qualities that keep

5   tourists and locals coming back for more. A long soak in an onsen can leave you feeling reborn, like you **don't have a care in the world**.

Onsens are more than just relaxing, though. They are a part of Japanese culture, and have a spiritual element as well. Most of them are shared, which means you'll be close to other bathers. When visiting an onsen, you should

10   be careful not to bother anyone by breaking the rules. Here are a few tips:

1. Respect the spring. Remember to shower before and after entering the onsen. When bathing in a shared onsen, never use soap or shampoo.

2. Respect other bathers. Soaking in an onsen is a spiritual experience for many people. Splashing, swearing, and loud noises are **frowned on** by

15   locals.

⌃ Many onsens don't allow people with tattoos to bathe.

« shower stall

» hot spring (onsen)

3. Respect the dress code. Swimsuits are usually not allowed at an onsen. A small towel will be provided for washing in the shower stall. This towel can be used to cover up when going to and from the onsen.

4. No tattoos. Many onsens don't allow people with tattoos to bathe, so if you have one you might be out of luck.

Questions

_____ 1. What is the main idea of this reading?
  a. Onsens are popular among tourists in Japan.
  b. Onsens are an important part of Japanese culture.
  c. Onsens don't let people with tattoos bathe.
  d. Onsens can be found all over Japan.

_____ 2. Which of the following is not a rule for bathing in an onsen?
  a. Don't wear a swimsuit.   b. Bring your own shampoo.
  c. Don't splash.   d. Shower before bathing.

_____ 3. What does it mean that the locals "**frown on**" loud noises?
  a. Only locals can make loud noises.
  b. Loud noises are a part of onsen culture.
  c. Loud noises make the locals upset.
  d. Locals aren't allowed to talk.

_____ 4. According to the article, which of the following is probably true?
  a. Most Japanese people live in onsens.
  b. Guests are allowed to swim laps in onsens.
  c. Foreign tourists aren't allowed to visit onsens.
  d. Tattoos are viewed negatively in Japan.

_____ 5. What does it mean if you "**don't have a care in the world**"?
  a. You are not worried about anything.
  b. You are hot and uncomfortable.
  c. You are trying something for the first time.
  d. You are learning about a new culture.

37 A Cappella Competitio

Do you love to sing?
Come and show off your talents at the

Chilton Youth *A Cappella*
Competition

5 ❯ *October 20th, 11:00—17:00*
❯ *Edward Greatcoat Theater, Sealey Road, Chilton*

❯ *Rules*

Please remember that this is an *a cappella* competition!

No instruments or recorded music will be allowed.

10 Competitors may sing published or original songs in any style.

Competitors must be between eight and 15 years old.

There are four categories:

❯ Solo (8—11 years old)   ❯ Solo (12—15 years old)

❯ Group (8—11 years old)   ❯ Group (12—15 years old)

15 ★ Competitors under 12 years old must stay with a
    parent or other adult at all times.

⌄ competitors

Questions

_____ 1. What is the purpose of this reading?

     a. To invite people to a concert at the Chilton School of Music.

     b. To inform young people about a singing competition.

     c. To encourage more visitors to come to the Edward Greatcoat Theate

     d. To offer free singing lessons with a famous voice coach.

_____ 2. What does "solo" mean?

     a. Clever.　　**b.** Alone.　　　　**c.** Usual.　　**d.** Young.

_____ 3. What does "these" mean?

     a. Showers.　　**b.** Instruments.　　**c.** Tickets.　　**d.** Music lessons.

★ Each competitor must pay an entry fee of $10.

★ Winners will receive $500 and a course of 20 lessons with famous voice coach Vickie Leonard.

★ Winners will be decided by three judges from the Chilton School of Music. Their decision is final.

❯ Additional information

★ Please arrive at the Edward Greatcoat Theater between 09:00 and 10:00 to register, as the competition will start at 11:00. The parking lot has limited spaces so you are advised to come as early as possible.

★ Shared dressing rooms with showers will be provided for all competitors.

★ Tickets to watch the competition are available at the theater from October 1st. There is no charge for **these**, but again, spaces are limited.

« solo

⌄ instruments

____ 4. What time does the event start?

    a. 9 a.m.   **b.** 10 a.m.

    c. 11 a.m.   **d.** Midday.

____ 5. Which of the following is true?

    a. You shouldn't try to argue with the judges.

    b. You can't park your car at the theater.

    c. You shouldn't go into the theater dressing rooms.

    d. You can't sing a song you wrote yourself.

George Psalmanazar
(c.1679–1763)

» Psalmanazar's
book

38 George Psalmanazar: 38 The Fake Formosan

In January of 1704, **the entire city of London** was talking about

one man—George Psalmanazar. He was a native of Formosa (modern-day

Taiwan), and he was the first man from that faraway country ever to visit

Britain. Or was he? He had blond hair and blue eyes; he certainly didn't look

5   Asian. And though the language he spoke certainly sounded foreign, it would

have **made little sense** to anyone from the real Formosa. But in 18th-

century London, hardly anyone had ever heard of Formosa, let alone seen a

person from that island.

To silence the few doubters that there were, Psalmanazar wrote a book.

10   Over 288 pages, Psalmanazar described the language, religion, politics, and

customs of his "native land." To play up to Western expectations, he made

many strange claims. For example, he claimed that each year Formosans

sacrificed 18,000 young boys to their cruel god. He also claimed that men

« Formosan funeral
procession from
Psalmanazar's
*Description of
Formosa* (1704), p

were allowed to kill and eat their wives if they suspected them

15 of cheating!

The book sold spectacularly at first, but, as with everything, people slowly grew tired of George Psalmanazar. Life after that was difficult for him; he became poor, sick, and later addicted to drugs. He died in 1763 after a long life of hardship,

20 a quiet man full of regret about the lies he had told. In his autobiography, which came out after his death, he confessed everything—everything, that is, except his real name.

Questions

_____ 1. What is the article about?
   a. A faraway island.   **b.** Eighteenth-century London.
   c. A famous liar.   **d.** A strange language.

_____ 2. What was not false about George Psalmanazar?
   a. His language.   **b.** His looks.
   c. His name.   **d.** His nationality.

_____ 3. What does it mean if something "makes little sense" to you ?
   a. You think it's funny.   **b.** You don't like how it sounds.
   c. You don't understand it. **d.** You think it sounds beautiful.

_____ 4. What can we guess about the people of 18th-century London?
   a. They loved hearing strange stories about foreign lands.
   b. Most of them had traveled widely in Asia.
   c. They hated anyone from a foreign country.
   d. They thought anyone with blue eyes was a foreigner.

_____ 5. What does the writer mean by "the entire city of London"?
   a. All the books in London.   **b.** All the buildings in London.
   c. All the people in London.   **d.** The city government of London.

39 Finding the Perfect Home

🏠 Listing 1: Here Comes the Sun

Want to get away from it all, but not go *too* far? Well, we have the home for you. Located at the top of Yangming Mountain, this beautiful home has windows that just

5   soak up the sunshine. In total it has three bedrooms, two bathrooms, and a traditional kitchen. There is also a large backyard with a view of the city. Perfect for a young family.

🏠 Listing 2: A Real Fixer-Upper

This apartment is a real steal for the right buyer. Some

10   might be **put off** by the age of the building, the cracked walls, and the water damage on the roof, but not you! You're a true handyman who can fix it up and make a pile of money doing it. Located in North District, this apartment has two bedrooms and one bathroom. It has no kitchen, though.

⌃ tennis court

⌄ cracked wall

🏠 Listing 3: The Heart of the City

This is the perfect home for a trader who's used to wheeling and dealing in the big city. Located in the heart of downtown, this three-bedroom apartment is brand new, complete with top-of-the-line modern appliances. The building also has a pool, tennis courts, and visitor parking.

« backyard

appliances

Listing 4: Country Living

They say that life is simpler in the country, so why not come and find out for yourself? This huge house has four bedrooms, three bathrooms, and a three-car garage. It also has its own private lake. Perfect for retiring in luxury and comfort.

25

Questions

1. What is this reading about?
   a. Finding a home.
   b. Fixing up apartments.
   c. Living in the city.
   d. Raising a family.

2. Which of the following is not true about Listing 3?
   a. It's located in the city.
   b. The building has a tennis court.
   c. It's in a new building.
   d. Visitor parking is not included.

3. What does it mean that some people might be "put off" by the age of the building in Listing 2?
   a. It will cause them to lose interest.
   b. It will make them want to buy it.
   c. They won't think it's important.
   d. They will ask more questions about it.

4. Which of the listings is probably the cheapest?
   a. Listing 1.   b. Listing 2.   c. Listing 3.   d. Listing 4.

5. Which picture is listing 4?
   a.   b.   c.   d.

40 TV Planet: Program Guide for Friday, 6th September

Have you had a busy week? Are you planning a quiet night at home? Only TV Planet gives you information for *every* channel, *every* day.

5 Whether you're into movies, cooking, or traveling, we're sure you'll find something to interest you.

Our TV guide is now interactive! Click on any program to get more

10 information.

14:00
Tennis: US Open
Catch up with the women's singles fin and other action from the last 24 hour

16:00
Children's Hour
Cartoons and educational programs for the under-11s.

17:00
My Perfect Home
Three **interior designers** offer ideas for improving your home. Tonight: kitchens.

Questions

_____ 1. What does the passage help us with?
   a. Watching programs online.
   b. Choosing something to watch.
   c. Buying a new television.
   d. Finding reviews of new movies

_____ 2. Which picture is probably from *Danger After Dark*?

a.
b.
c.
d.

17:30

Get Away!

This week, the team travels to Morocco to camp under the stars.

18:30

Evening News

Bryan Constance presents international, national, and local news stories.

19:00

Dream Street

Weekly series. Lewis is keeping a secret from Tessa; will it break them up?

19:30

Captain Cook

More cooking advice from top French chef Antoine Lambert. Tonight: desserts.

20:00

My Boyfriend is a Bear

Comedy movie from 2012 starring Nick Langton and Maria Cavelli.

22:00

News Focus

Angela Morton discusses the week's big stories with special guests.

23:00

Danger After Dark

Police drama. Who is the strange man following Emily?

---

3. What does an "interior designer" do?
   a. Change the look of rooms in your house.
   b. Teach young people how to cook.
   c. Help you to improve your garden.
   d. Organize travel tickets and hotels.

4. What is *Get Away!* about?
   a. Fashion.   b. Sports.   c. Vacations.   d. Cars.

5. Julia is a fan of romantic dramas. Which program would she probably enjoy?
   a. *Captain Cook.*
   b. *My Perfect Home.*
   c. *News Focus.*
   d. *Dream Street.*

Dear Mr. Phelps,

It is our pleasure to tell you that you've been accepted into the engineering program at Stockton University. We look forward to seeing you in September.

5 You have every reason to be on **cloud nine** about getting into Stockton. This year we received an unprecedented number of applications for the engineering program. Yours was one of 100 successful ones out of a pool of over 10,000! This is a vote of confidence in your background. You have the education, experience, and personal qualities that we look for in a 10 Stockton engineer.

Your next step is to fill out the intent to register and mail it back to our office. Then you will be officially registered for the autumn term. Our records also indicate that you're an international student. Don't forget to complete the meal plan and housing 15 forms and get them back to us as soon as possible.

After the paperwork is done, the real fun begins. You don't need to wait until September to get to know Stockton. There is a Facebook group that helps students introduce themselves and network before the term begins. You may even find a new friend or roommate before the first day of class.

20 You should be very proud of your success.

Warm regards,

Jimmy Smits

fill out

1. What is this letter about?
    a. Life at Stockton University.
    b. How to network using Facebook.
    c. Getting into a university.
    d. How to write an application.

_____ 2. Which of the following is not true about Mr. Phelps?
    a. He has already mailed his intent to register.
    b. He is an international student.
    c. He has been accepted into Stockton University.
    d. He has a good educational background.

paperwork

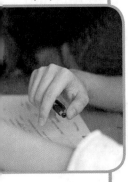

_____ 3. What does it mean to be on "**cloud nine**"?
    a. You don't know what to do next.
    b. You're a little scared.
    c. You're very happy.
    d. You have lots of friends.

_____ 4. Which of the following is probably true about Mr. Phelps?
    a. He's always wanted to be a journalist.
    b. He's going to live on campus in September.
    c. His was the best application Stockton received.
    d. He doesn't have enough money to go to Stockton.

« roommate

introduce

_____ 5. What is Mr. Phelps studying to become?
    a.    b.

    c.    d.

Vote for Sam

Attention People of Parkdale:

I, Sam Smith, am running for president in the upcoming Parkdale Community Association elections. I have not taken this decision lightly. I would rather spend my golden years of retirement like anyone else, drinking green tea and watching baseball. However, I can no longer stand by and watch as Parkdale is **laid to waste** by wild youths and poor leadership. It's time we got the law and order that we deserve. If I am elected, I promise to pass the following community bylaws:

- All youths must be off the streets by 10 p.m. unless they have a special pass from the community association.

- A community-wide ban on music outdoors. This includes joggers and bikers with those little radios.

- Air conditioning will be turned up in all community areas.

« playgro

- The playground will be torn down and turned into an exercise area for the elderly.

- Anyone found not cleaning up after h or her dog will pay a "doo-doo tax" of $250. We will also make the names o these people public, so everyone will know who's **breaking** the rules.

With me as your president, Parkdale won't just be cleaner and quieter; it will make sense again. So I ask the fair people of Parkdale to make the right choice and vote for Sam!

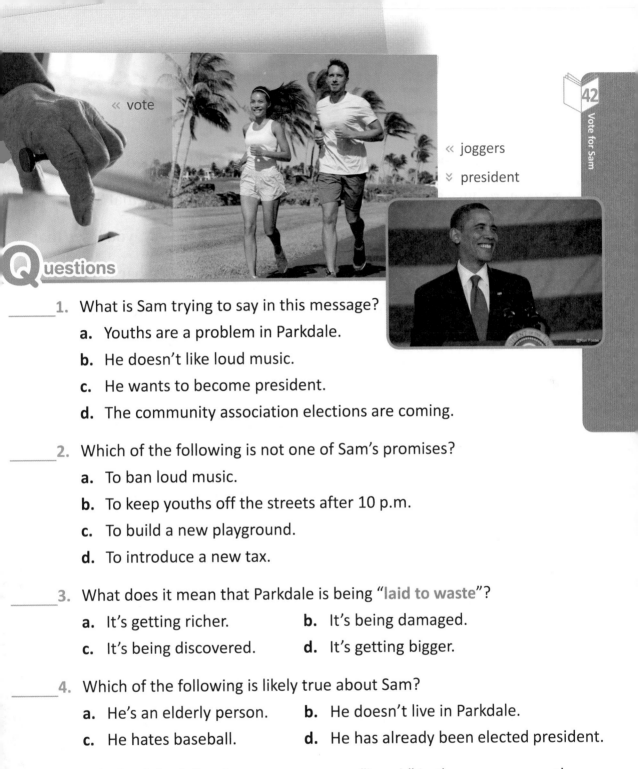

« vote

« joggers

« president

Questions

_____ 1. What is Sam trying to say in this message?

a. Youths are a problem in Parkdale.

b. He doesn't like loud music.

c. He wants to become president.

d. The community association elections are coming.

_____ 2. Which of the following is not one of Sam's promises?

a. To ban loud music.

b. To keep youths off the streets after 10 p.m.

c. To build a new playground.

d. To introduce a new tax.

_____ 3. What does it mean that Parkdale is being "laid to waste"?

a. It's getting richer.   b. It's being damaged.

c. It's being discovered.   d. It's getting bigger.

_____ 4. Which of the following is likely true about Sam?

a. He's an elderly person.   b. He doesn't live in Parkdale.

c. He hates baseball.   d. He has already been elected president.

_____ 5. Which of the following sentences uses "break" in the same way as the article?

a. After the storm, the sun broke through the clouds.

b. Tim broke his new toy just a day after it was given to him.

c. John broke the law and paid for it with two years of his life.

d. He broke a twenty-dollar bill to make change.

43 | The Whole Is Greater Than Its Parts (43)

The next time your mom tells you to stop playing video games, just say you're busy studying an ancient art. After all, the original Super Mario is like any other mosaic. If you look at him closely, you'll see that he's made up of tiny, different-colored dots. Take a step back and these
5 dots blend together to form the image of a Goomba-stomping plumber.

Mosaic art has been around for thousands of years. It started in the eighth century BC as a way to make patterns on roads out of different-colored stones. By the fourth century BC, the Greeks were making mosaics showing people and animals. The Romans then **built on**
10 the technique and began using mosaics to decorate the floors of their houses. A popular mosaic in ancient Rome was a picture of a black dog, which was meant to keep away thieves.

Mosaics have also been an important form of religious art. Some of the earliest Christian art came in the form of Byzantine mosaics of
15 Jesus and the apostles. Islamic artists cannot show humans or animals in their work, so they used mosaics to form complex shapes and patterns.

It's not just in video games that the mosaic is **still kicking** today. Mosaics can be found in galleries around the world, and computers are
20 being used to make mosaics from photographs. It seems likely that this art form will survive another thousand years.

» mosaic architecture in Spain

^ Roman mosaic of an animal

^ Byzantine mosaic of Jesus washing the apostles' feet, at the Monreale Cathedral, Italy

Questions

_____ 1. What is this article about?

    a. A video game.

    b. An art form.

    c. An old painting.

    d. A religion.

_____ 2. How did the Romans use mosaics?

    a. To make patterns on roads.

    b. To show complex shapes and patterns.

    c. To decorate their houses.

    d. To make pictures of Jesus.

_____ 3. What does it mean that the Romans "**built on**" the Greeks' technique?

    a. They copied it.

    b. They improved it.

    c. They gave it up.

    d. They couldn't understand it.

_____ 4. Which of the following is likely an example of a popular painting in Islamic art?

    a. A busy city street.

    b. A bear at a river.

    c. A family sitting by a fire.

    d. A pattern of triangles.

_____ 5. What does it mean that the mosaic is "**still kicking**" today?

    a. It is alive and well.

    b. It is almost forgotten.

    c. It makes people angry.

    d. It has totally changed.

44

A Spiritual Journey

Yoga is an ancient practice that started in India and has since spread across the world. It is not just a set of exercises meant to help you get in shape. It is a state of mind, one that carries with it a deep and rewarding spiritual well-being. Some even say yoga can help cure diseases like cancer. While science has yet to confirm these claims, one thing is certain: to master yoga is to know inner peace.

I have wanted to write a book and share my own experiences with yoga for a long time. You now hold **the fruit of my labor** in your hands. I hope that it will help you take the same journey that I once did.

Table of Contents

Part 1 The History of Yoga		Part 3 Yoga Exercises	
The First Yoga Teachers	1	The Basics	65
Early Yoga	5	Camel	67
The Vedic Period	11	Tree	68
The Middle Ages	24	Bow	69
Modern Yoga	34	Caterpillar	70
Part 2 The Spiritual Side of Yoga		Downward Dog	71
		Triangle	72
Meditation	49	**Part 4 Conclusion**	
Living Your Own Life	60	Parting Thoughts	75
The Road to Peace	62	Index	76

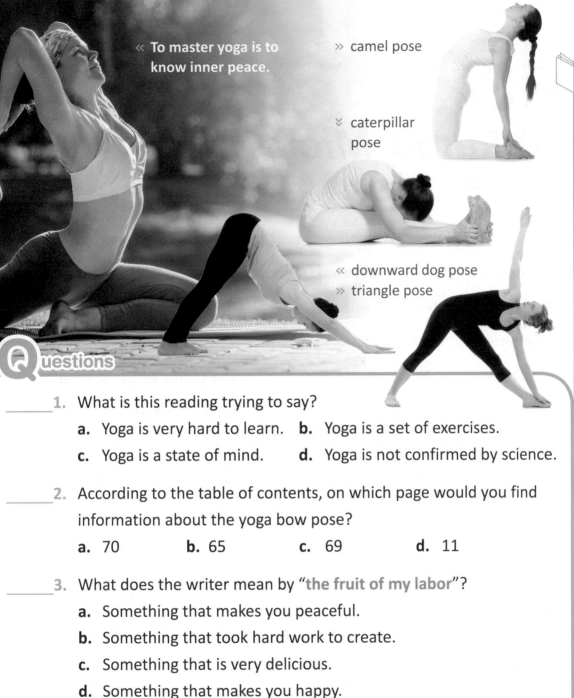

« To master yoga is to know inner peace.

» camel pose

caterpillar pose

« downward dog pose
» triangle pose

Questions

_____ 1. What is this reading trying to say?

    a. Yoga is very hard to learn. **b.** Yoga is a set of exercises.

    c. Yoga is a state of mind.   **d.** Yoga is not confirmed by science.

_____ 2. According to the table of contents, on which page would you find information about the yoga bow pose?

    a. 70   **b.** 65   **c.** 69   **d.** 11

_____ 3. What does the writer mean by "**the fruit of my labor**"?

    a. Something that makes you peaceful.

    b. Something that took hard work to create.

    c. Something that is very delicious.

    d. Something that makes you happy.

_____ 4. "The earliest yoga teachings appeared sometime during the third century BC." In which part of the book would you find this sentence?

    a. Part 1.   **b.** Part 2.   **c.** Part 3.   **d.** Part 4.

_____ 5. If someone wants to learn more about meditation exercises, which part should he or she read?

    a. Part 1.   **b.** Part 2.   **c.** Part 3.   **d.** Part 4.

45

» *Mikania micrantha*
(cc by Jeevan Jose, Kerala, India)

Mikania Micrantha —Invader!

by **Green Glenda**

Hi, nature lovers! Welcome to this week's nature column. This week I wanted to talk about an interesting phenomenon—
5 invasive species. Now, we all know how important it is to protect nature, but sometimes nature can be a danger to itself! Invasive species are plants that come from
10 abroad, spread, and cause harm to local plants. Case in point: the plant *Mikania micrantha*, also known as the "mile-a-minute weed," which is taking over
15 Taiwan's nature parks.

The plant, which originally comes from South America, grows at an incredible speed, hence **its nickname**. After flowering,
20 the plant also produces a large number of very light seeds that are easily spread by the wind,

Questions

_____ 1. What is the column mainly about?
    a. A plant that kills other plants.   **b.** How plants spread to different p
    c. The plants of South America.   **d.** Helping out at Taiwan's nature p

_____ 2. What is said about *Mikania micrantha*?
    a. It grows very slowly.   **b.** It produces only a few seeds.
    c. It's a foreign plant.   **d.** It avoids other plants as it sprea

_____ 3. What does the writer mean by "**its nickname**"?
    a. Green cancer.   **b.** *Mikania micrantha*.
    c. Mile-a-minute weed.   **d.** Mother Nature.

animals, insects, or humans. In addition, sections of the plant can

25 take root independently, helping it spread over a large area.

Mikania micrantha is so unwelcome because as it spreads, it clings to other plants until it

30 covers them completely. This effectively chokes the plants, blocking their sunlight and slowly killing them.

Things have gotten so bad

35 in Taiwan that the government has had to hire volunteers to help clear *Mikania micrantha* from heavily affected areas. It's strange to think that even though we

40 humans do a lot of damage to the environment, Mother Nature does sometimes **shoot herself in the foot** as well! Get in touch with your nearest nature park and find

45 out if there's anything you can do to help fight this green cancer!

As *Mikania micrantha* spreads, it clings to other plants until it covers them completely. (cc by Ks.mini)

_____ 4. What is Green Glenda's opinion of *Mikania micrantha*?

   a. We should leave it alone.   b. We should help it spread.

   c. We should grow it for food.   d. We should stop its spreading.

_____ 5. What does it mean if you "**shoot yourself in the foot**"?

   a. You do something good for others.

   b. You cause problems for yourself.

   c. You hurt yourself to avoid doing something.

   d. You do something no one would expect.

46 SARS and MERS, Meet the WHO

» WHO logo

In 2015, a virus called the Middle East Respiratory Syndrome (MER[S])
spread from Saudi Arabia to South Korea. By early June, it had infected
over 1,333 people, resulting in at least 471 deaths.

This is not the first time the world has seen a dangerous new diseas[e].
In 2002, the Severe Acute Respiratory Syndrome (SARS) appeared,
spreading throughout Asia and beyond. Like MERS, SARS was a
coronavirus, the same kind that causes the common cold. By the time
SARS **fizzled out**, it had
killed over 774 people.

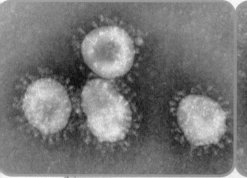
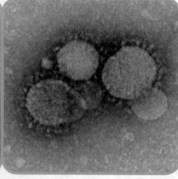

The sudden appearance o[f]
new and dangerous diseases
is a big threat. In the past,
diseases could only spread a[s]

⌃ SARS coronavirus   ⌃ MERS coronavirus

far as humans could take them. An outbreak might affect a city or regio[n]
15 but it wouldn't spread further because travel was so slow. Nowadays th[e]
situation is different. A person infected with MERS can fly to the other
side of the world in ten hours. If he or she infects someone else on the
plane, that person might fly somewhere
else. In mere days we could have a global
20 pandemic **on our hands.**

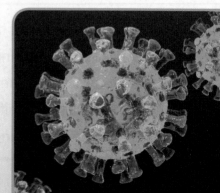

» 3D MERS virus image (cc by Scinceside)

Luckily there is a global organization fighting this global threat. The United Nations World Health Organization (WHO) is always first on the scene when a new disease appears. It acts as a command center, sending doctors, testing patients, and issuing travel warnings if necessary. Whether it's SARS, MERS, or whatever comes next, the WHO has the tools to beat the diseases of the 21st century.

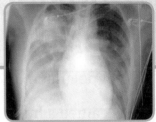

≪ A chest X-ray showing increased opacity in both lungs, indicative of pneumonia, in a patient with SARS (Wikipedia)

Questions

_____ 1. What is this reading trying to say?
   a. MERS is a dangerous disease.
   b. SARS spread throughout Asia.
   c. Diseases can spread on airplanes.
   d. Global diseases need a global solution.

_____ 2. Which of the following is not true about MERS?
   a. It infected over 1,333 people.   b. It is a coronavirus.
   c. It killed over 774 people.   d. It first appeared in Saudi Arabia.

_____ 3. What does it mean to have a situation "on our hands"?
   a. We are responsible for dealing with it.
   b. No one knows what to do about it.
   c. It can be ignored.
   d. It has never happened before.

_____ 4. Which of the following is probably another duty of the WHO?
   a. Tracking people who come into contact with dangerous diseases.
   b. Inventing and testing new diseases for world governments.
   c. Flying people out of dangerous areas where war has broken out.
   d. Giving food to poor children who have nothing to eat.

_____ 5. What does the writer mean by saying SARS "fizzled out"?
   a. It spread to more and more countries.
   b. It changed into another type of disease.
   c. It slowed down and then disappeared.
   d. It became more and more dangerous.

47. Smog: Choking the World's Cities

A documentary by Chinese **environmentalist** Chai Jing has gained a huge amount of attention since being posted online. The film deals with China's increasingly serious problem with smog. But what is smog? And is it only a Chinese problem?

5   Smog is, in fact, a big problem for many modern cities. It is a type of air pollution that causes serious health problems such as lung disease, cancer, and even abnormal births. Here are some of the main causes of smog:

⌄ smog

Questions

_____ 1. What is the main subject of the article?
- **a.** The weather in Los Angeles.
- **b.** A new movie about the environment.
- **c.** A dangerous form of air pollution.
- **d.** Farming methods in Asia.

_____ 2. What is said about smog in the article?
- **a.** It's a problem unique to China.
- **b.** Sunny weather helps clear smog.
- **c.** Smog is not caused by burning coal.
- **d.** Smog is bad for people's health.

Burning Coal

Classic smog is a result of the large amounts of dirty smoke produced by burning coal. This type of smog is very thick and can be green, yellow, or black. The worst-ever wave of this killer smog struck London in 1952, when 12,000 people died over the course of a couple of days.

Pollution From Cars

Pollution from car exhausts and/or industrial engines causes a primary smog, which is then made worse by sunlight. The sunlight reacts with the pollutants in the air to create even worse chemical pollutants. This type of smog is a particular problem in very sunny cities, such as Los Angeles on the west coast of the United States.

Farming

The practice of clearing land for farming by burning vegetation in parts of Southeast Asia has resulted in a large blanket of smog that hangs over the region. It has become known as the Asian brown cloud.

_____ 3. What is an "environmentalist"?
   a. A person who cares about the natural world.
   b. A person who writes for a magazine.
   c. A person who cares for sick people.
   d. A person who travels all over the world.

_____ 4. Which of these would help keep smog levels down?
   a. Clearing more land for farms.
   b. Having fewer cars on the road.
   c. Burning oil instead of coal.
   d. Closing factories when it's raining.

_____ 5. What does "the region" mean?
   a. London.
   b. Los Angeles.
   c. China.
   d. Southeast Asia.

48

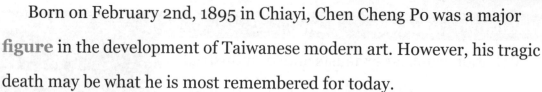

» Chen Cheng Po
(1895 — 1947)

Chen Cheng Po

Born on February 2nd, 1895 in Chiayi, Chen Cheng Po was a major **figure** in the development of Taiwanese modern art. However, his tragic death may be what he is most remembered for today.

Growing up under Japanese rule, Chen left Taiwan in 1924 to study at
5 the Tokyo School of Fine Arts. Two years later, his painting *Street of Chiayi* was displayed at the Imperial Art Exhibition in Tokyo. Chen was the first Taiwanese artist to have his work shown at this prestigious exhibition.

Questions

_____1. What is the main idea of this reading?
- **a.** Chen Cheng Po's death was very tragic.
- **b.** Chen Cheng Po was an important Taiwanese modern artist.
- **c.** Chen Cheng Po's paintings are very expensive to buy.
- **d.** Many of Chen Cheng Po's works were displayed in 2014.

_____2. In what sort of style did Chen Cheng Po paint?
- **a.** A traditional Taiwanese style.
- **b.** A modern Western style.
- **c.** A combined Taiwanese and foreign style.
- **d.** A traditional Japanese style.

_____3. Which of the following sentences uses "**figure**" in the same way as the reading?
- **a.** The sales figures don't look too good this year.
- **b.** She had the long, thin figure of a model.
- **c.** He was a key figure in the government long before his election.
- **d.** My brother's favorite toy is a small Spider-Man figure.

Self-Portrait (1927)

Chen's work combines traditional Taiwanese elements with the modern foreign painting styles he saw in his many travels. Several of his pieces have sold for high prices at auction in recent years.

In addition to drawing and painting, Chen wanted to advance artistic education in Taiwan, and was a professor himself.

During the 228 uprising in 1947, Chen was sent to negotiate a peace agreement between Chiayi citizens and Kuomintang troops. Tragically, he was shot dead, aged only 52.

⌄ *Street Scene on a Summer Day* (1927) was selected for the eighth Empire Art Exhibition.

In 2014, an exhibition marking Chen's 120th birthday toured Taiwan, China, and Japan. Nearly 500 of the painter's works and personal items were on display for a new generation to discover. **It** was an overdue celebration of this important artist and teacher whose life and death reflect the history of modern Taiwan.

_____ 4. Why was Chen Cheng Po probably killed?
   a. Because he was an artist.
   b. Because he had studied in Japan.
   c. Because of his ideas about education.
   d. Because of his ideas about government.

_____ 5. What does "**it**" mean?
   a. A famous painting by Chen Cheng Po.
   b. A personal item of Chen Cheng Po's.
   c. An exhibition of Chen Cheng Po's work.
   d. Chen Cheng Po's 120th birthday.

⌃ *Street of Chiayi* (1926) was exhibited at Japan's seventh Imperial Art Exhibition.

49

The Dogs of War

The terrible experiences of war often stay with soldiers long after they leave the battlefield. Many ex-soldiers develop a condition called post-traumatic stress disorder (PTSD). Sufferers experience nightly bad dreams and panic attacks and may

5   become moody, jumpy, or depressed. But it's not just human soldiers who suffer from PTSD. Dogs used by the military suffer too.

Because of their sensitive noses and excellent instincts, dogs are being used more and more by the military. They are used to find bombs, track down enemy fighters, and clear buildings of dangers before human

10   soldiers enter. They're excellent soldiers, well-trained and disciplined, following orders without question. But dogs are also very emotional animals, who form strong relationships with the soldiers they serve beside.

During their tours of duty, military dogs experience the same types of traumatic events as regular soldiers. Experiences such as losing a

15   fellow soldier, getting wounded, or coming under heavy fire cause these brave animals great stress. And they bring the emotional scars of these experiences home with them **when their duty is done**.

The treatment for these dogs is, again, similar to that for humans.

< military dog

Dogs with **mild** PTSD can be cured with a period of rest. More serious cases require drugs to help them stay calm. Some dogs, unfortunately, never fully recover and must be re-homed with loving families who understand their condition. 20

It's sad that the wars of men hurt not only people, but also man's best friend. 25

Questions

_____ 1. What is the message of the reading?
   a. The military uses dogs to carry out many difficult tasks.
   b. Dogs are affected by war much as people are.
   c. Dogs form strong relationships with their human owners.
   d. Dogs, by their very nature, make excellent soldiers.

_____ 2. Which of the following is not a sign of PTSD?
   a. Having bad dreams.   **b.** Experiencing sudden changes in emotion.
   c. Always feeling on edge.   **d.** Developing a good sense of smell.

_____ 3. What does the phrase "**when their duty is done**" mean here?
   a. When they complete their training.
   b. When they don't have to fight anymore.
   c. When they are fully recovered.
   d. When they go into battle.

⌃ PTSD sufferers may become moody, jumpy, or depressed.

_____ 4. Why is it possible for dogs to suffer PTSD?
   a. They follow orders without question.
   b. Their senses are better than those of humans.
   c. They experience emotions very strongly.
   d. They receive lots of hard training.

_____ 5. Which of these describes something "**mild**"?
   a. It's not very serious.   **b.** It puts your life in danger.
   c. There is no cure for it.   **d.** Nobody understands it.

50 A Green Skyline

» All new rooftops must be covered with plants or solar panels in France.

In March 2015, the French government passed a law that is set to change the face of France's cities. The law states that the roofs of all new buildings in commercial zones must be covered in part with either plants or solar panels.

⌃ rooftop garden

The benefits of these so-called rooftop gardens are

5 many. They will help cut the amount of energy needed for heating and cooling the buildings in summer and winter. The plants on green roofs will help filter unpleasant gases, thus cleaning the polluted city air. The soil used to grow the plants will also help retain

10 rainwater. This will make problems with runoff—such as the flooding of sewer systems—a lot rarer. In addition, these rooftop gardens will give birds a place to nest in an otherwise unsuitable city environment. And of course they will create new community areas in cities where space is limited.

French environmentalists wanted the law to state that plants should

15 completely cover the roofs of all new buildings. However, **as a first step**, the government decided to limit the law's power so that only commercial buildings would be affected. The government also suggested giving businesses the choice of fitting solar panels onto their roofs to generate their own power rather than growing plants. **This** would give businesses the chance to cut

20 their own carbon footprints.

France is now one of many countries, including Germany, Australia, and Canada, that use green roofs

110 to lower their negative effect on the environment.

« solar panel

Questions

_____ 1. What is the article about?
- **a.** Making French cities more beautiful.
- **b.** Getting more tourists to visit French cities.
- **c.** Creating more businesses in French cities.
- **d.** Making French cities more environmentally friendly.

_____ 2. Rooftop gardens help do which of the following?
- **a.** Clean cities' dirty air.
- **b.** Create homes for homeless people.
- **c.** Keep unwanted animals away.
- **d.** Provide fresh, clean drinking water.

_____ 3. What does "**This**" mean?
- **a.** Forcing businesses to grow plants.
- **b.** Allowing businesses to create their own energy.
- **c.** Limiting the new law's power.
- **d.** Making sure that only commercial buildings are affected.

_____ 4. What can you guess from the final paragraph?
- **a.** France is the first-ever country to have green roofs.
- **b.** The French people were against green roofs to begin with.
- **c.** Setting up green roofs is a growing worldwide movement.
- **d.** The French government doesn't care about the environment.

_____ 5. According to the article, the French government limited the green roof law to commercial buildings "**as a first step**." What does this suggest about the government's plans?
- **a.** It is considering passing similar laws for other types of buildings.
- **b.** It wants to stop similar laws from ever being passed.
- **c.** It wants to limit the current law's powers even more.
- **d.** It wants to build as many green roofs as possible as soon as possible.

« rainwater

TRANSLATION

1 內在美

貝絲:嘿,潔西卡,妳在嗎?

潔西卡:我在啊,怎麼啦?

貝絲:我剛跟我媽大吵一架,吵得有夠兇的,我們兩個誰也不讓步。

潔西卡:怎麼會這樣!妳們是吵什麼?

貝絲:還不是老樣子,她逮到我化妝出門。我已經要踏出後門了,結果被她叫進來,然後她看到我畫眼線就翻臉。

潔西卡:想像得到她的反應,尤其是經過上週末的事。

貝絲:她對這件事的反應根本是瘋了。我14歲,幾乎要成年。以妳為例好了,妳媽讓妳在12歲的時候就化妝。

潔西卡:是沒錯,但妳有沒有發現,我幾乎沒在化妝。

貝絲:其實我有注意到,怎麼回事呢?如果我媽這麼酷,我一定會常常化妝。

潔西卡:我知道當大家都在化妝,只有妳沒做這件事的感覺有多糟。不過化妝其實沒有那麼好玩,事實上,還有點麻煩。

貝絲:什麼意思呢?

潔西卡:化妝和卸妝都很花時間,而且我們不應該靠化妝來感受自己漂亮的一面,而是要著重內在美,妳的個人魅力才重要。

貝絲:說得好!那這樣的意思是,妳的化妝品可以給我嗎?

2 楊家的預算計畫

擬訂預算計畫是讓家庭收支狀態井然有序的好方法。以楊家為例,楊先生不喜歡一開始就訂定預算的做法,他表示:「我還寧願去看牙醫」不過,當楊太太想出了一個全家都會同意的目標時,楊先生竟然改觀了。這個目標就是為了新公寓省吃儉用,讓楊家的每個孩子都能擁有自己的房間。

楊家人先從記帳開始,這是擬定任何預算計畫的第一步,因為有助於你判斷開支的流向。一旦清楚開支,就能安排下個月的預算。楊家人多年來累積儲蓄的習慣,很快就能買下那間更大的公寓了。

3 登上高空

今天的發文內容可能有點不符我平常的發文風格,請大家忍耐一下吧。某天我吃午餐的時候,聽到有人在聊無人空中載具(簡稱UAV)。聽起來很酷,所以我決定搜尋這方面的資訊,超開心我有這麼做!

是這樣的:UAV是指不需駕駛員的飛行器,包括大型的軍用等級UAV,例如美軍使用的無人機,可發射火箭與炸毀建物,但我們不喜歡這種。而所謂的小型UAV或稱「私人無人機」比較好,因為能用在更和平的用途,例如在私人無人機上架設照相機,從高空俯瞰拍攝照片。或者純粹享受遙控飛行機器人的感覺,光是操控無人機就是件很酷的事。有人說,使用遙控器駕駛UAV

比世上任何一款電玩遊戲都還有趣。

　　雖然 UAV 目前仍要價不斐，但我想我會一頭栽入這個世界。我已經看中一款稱為「幻影」的無人機，頂部有四支螺旋槳，底部則有一架攝影機。但我覺得電池的部分是一個缺點，因為使用15分鐘就會耗盡電量，還需一小時才能充電完畢。

　　讀者們，意下如何呢？UAV 很棒，不是嗎？我該買一台嗎？請大家在下方發表意見！

 4　過海關

C：海關人員　**T：**遊客

C：先生，午安。您今天從哪裡搭機抵達這裡？

T：從曼谷。

C：好的。您在飛機上有拿到海關申報表嗎？

T：有的，在這裡。

C：謝謝您。「無需申報」。可以請您打開託運行李箱嗎？

T：好吧……打開了。

C：謝謝您。您有在泰國購買任何物品嗎？

T：只有這些 T 恤和紀念品而已，是要送朋友的禮物。有什麼問題嗎？

C：這些小東西沒有問題。您旅遊的時候是否有購買較高單價的物品？例如黃金或珠寶？

T：當然沒有。這類東西已經超越我的預算！

C：那水果或其他食品呢？

T：只有你現在看到的這包咖啡。

C：好的。可以請您打開登機箱嗎？

T：一定要嗎？外頭有人等著幫我接機。

C：先生，恐怕這是必要的程序，不會拖太久的。

T：好吧。

C：……呃，先生，這是什麼？

T：是一些糯米。我今天早上搭機前，在市場買的，其實我忘了自己有帶這個東西。

C：嗯，您不能將這項物品帶進台灣，因為沒有密封包裝。

T：你確定嗎？不過是一樣小東西。

C：抱歉，先生，我必須沒收。不過其他東西都沒有問題，您可以離開了。

T：謝謝，那你好好享用我的糯米吧！

 **5　門診時間表**

　　歡迎來到不需預約的晴溪診所。我們每週營業五天，每天固定有兩位醫師駐診為您服務。由四名醫師組成的本診所醫療團隊，看診經驗總計超過90年。我們亦提供必要時候的到府看診服務。不過，在您來電要求醫師出診前，請先確保您的健保涵蓋此類服務。

　　您可於下表查找各醫師的看診時間。雖然我們接受未預約的患者，但仍鼓勵您提早來電預約看診，以免向隅。

親愛的凱西：

　　妳還好嗎？！當我聽到妳的遭遇，妳都不曉得我有多驚恐。我當然還是很擔心，但還好妳的傷勢是不幸中的大幸。昨天早上我有去看妳，但妳還在睡覺，護士叫我不要吵醒妳。我留了一個小禮物給妳，我想妳現在已經看到了。希望妳喜歡，我知道史努比是妳最喜歡的卡通人物。

　　無論如何，我們都好想妳，但最想妳的人是我。少了妳這個八卦的開心果，上學一點都不好玩，而且放學回家後，我也提不起勁做任何事，沒有最好的朋友在身邊，生活有什麼意義呢？我們家還是會在星期六去海灘玩，但我想沒有妳陪伴，我一定玩得不開心。我們本來都好期待這次出遊，結果妳卻出了意外。爸媽每天都在問我妳的情況，他們也對於妳無法一起來玩感到遺憾。

　　好的，卡片都快被我寫滿了，該停筆囉。我發誓週末之前我還會再去探望妳。在那之前，妳就多休息，好好聽醫生的話，最重要的是……

　　　　趕快好起來喔！

妳永遠的摯友
喬伊絲

主持人：我們今天請到曾是童星的傑克‧柏寧根。大家還記得傑克演出過的老電視劇《誰才是老大？》嗎？他飾演可愛又調皮的大衛長達五季的時間。現在他是 Chili's 美式餐廳的服務生。哈囉，傑克！

傑克：哈囉，不好意思我不是要雞蛋裡挑骨頭，不過我其實是副店長。

主持人：很棒呀，傑克。可以請你跟我們分享，當年拍攝《誰才是老大？》的經歷嗎？

傑克：對一個七歲小孩來說，是個蠻奇怪的經驗。因為多數的同年齡小孩，都在遊樂場和朋友們玩耍，而我卻天天待在攝影棚拍片。就像年紀輕輕卻已經有份全職工作的感覺，我甚至沒去上學。

主持人：不過你那時等於大賺一筆，對不對？對一個小男孩來說一定很棒。

傑克：也不是這樣。我當時年紀太小，沒辦法好好規劃《誰才是老大？》的片酬。

主持人：太可惜了！你現在過得怎麼樣呢？從明星轉行變服務生的感覺一定有點怪。

傑克：其實也沒那麼糟。人生不如意事十之八九，重點是汲取經驗振作起來。

主持人：這樣的心態非常正面。你很棒，傑克。謝謝你光臨我們的節目，祝你在新事業領域大展鴻圖！

MAJOR LEAGUE BASEBALL

8 帶我去看球賽

　　美國職業棒球大聯盟(簡稱MLB)於1903年創立,可說是北美洲歷史最悠久的運動聯盟之一。有些人甚至認為,MLB家喻戶曉的程度,就像一提到蘋果派就會想到美國人一樣。許多美國人都有被父母帶去看球賽的快樂兒時回憶。

　　球賽門票費用不固定,票價漲跌的情況取決於星期幾開賽。星期五和週末的門票最昂貴,而星期三的門票最便宜,票價落差可說是天壤之別。與到場觀賞週六球賽相較下,週三去看球平均可省下23塊美金。對棒球迷而言,在平日有些閒暇時間還是有好處的!

9 大家都能是影評

約翰

14:15,發文者 約翰
大家有沒有看過《恐龍來襲》這部電影?超刺激的!這十年來的電影特效真的進步得不可思議。劇情好緊張!有一幕嚇死我,害我把手上的爆米花打翻,灑得旁邊的人身上都是。

茉莉

14:15 發文者 茉莉
我覺得這部電影應該改名為「睡意來襲」比較恰當。片中的女星是都怎麼回事?不是尖叫就是躲在角落等著英雄救美,我覺得大銀幕如果偶爾能呈現個性堅強的女性模範角色會比較好。

包柏

14:16 發文者 包柏
大家都有權發表影評!不過是部電影罷了,茉莉。我們看電影的目的在於忘掉現實生活與樂在其中。妳不用太認真,放輕鬆就好。

茉莉

14:20 發文者 茉莉
你說得簡單,包柏,每部電影裡都在尖叫哭鬧的又不是你們男生。你應該捫心自問,我們該怎麼引導年輕女孩。例如她們是要堅強獨立,抑或當個小鳥依人、需要男人拯救的女生?她們看到的電影情節確實會產生重大影響力。

10 請勿停車

此機車車主您好:

　　過去數週以來,我已經看您在此停車好幾次。不知您曉不曉得,這是私人停車位,您在此停車是違法的。

　　我知道在一位難求的這區看到空位,會讓人不假思索地先停再說。不過,請您將心比心,有時我結束11小時的輪班工作,卻無法停車在自家門口,導致我必須不斷繞著此街區找停車位。

　　非法停車在我居住的這棟大樓是十分嚴重的問題。很多鄰居不像我這麼仁慈，他們會省略警告，直接聯絡拖吊車。被拖吊的倒楣車主必須自費牽車，費用高達3000新台幣。我喜歡先提醒車主，希望車主能聽勸。

　　請您別再將愛車停放於此。如果您剛好看到有人也在做同樣的事，請轉告我的話。我衷心希望正面的規勸，會比聯絡拖吊車的方式好很多。

吉姆敬上

11 聖派屈克節遊行

　　超過50年的時間，聖派屈克節遊行一直是本城鎮引以為傲的傳統。此節日的用意在於向擁有建國貢獻的移民致敬，現已成為我們社區的重要節慶。大家每年均引頸期盼此活動的到來，只要到了融雪的時節，就知道聖派屈克節遊行即將來臨。

　　今年的遊行規模將名留青史，這是首次有其他城鎮的居民共襄盛舉，每個城鎮將建造自己的花車。活動當日，所有花車將沿著往常的路線遊行。遊行結束後，每個人都能投票選出自己最喜歡的花車，獲選的城鎮即可贏得「花車王」的頭銜，直到明年的遊行再次選出。

12 勇氣

人生的考驗總是不期而遇；
人生的考驗總是千變萬化。
因為我們都認為自己正氣凜然，能夠挺身而出抗爭，
所以我們都認為邪終不能勝正。
但真正面臨考驗時卻無法如此肯定，
而最終的結果可能令人難以接受。

勇氣，是推動歷史前進的一種精神；
勇氣，是我無從尋覓的一股精髓。

上星期，我在校園裡遇到了考驗，
以往我從不認為自己是個膽怯的人，
但當我看到四人霸凌一人，
我居然沒有伸出援手，而是轉身逃跑躲避。
現在他不再來上學，
他唯一的錯，只不過是沒有那些人愛「裝酷要帥」。

勇氣是如何抉擇，
誰該站出來，又是誰該轉身。

日子一天天過去，那位同學仍無蹤影。
我決定四處打聽，是否有人知道他的下落。
他是個獨行俠，幾乎沒有朋友。
不與人來往或打哈哈，彷彿自力更生。

他離開了，我害怕他不再回到學校。
假如我當時想辦法援助，將他拉回正軌就好了。
勇氣，你讓我付出好大的代價。
勇氣，你離開了我，如今我不知所措。

13 搶救我們的公園

所有格蘭戴爾的居民請注意

是時候齊心協力搶救我們所喜愛的公園了。許多人都知道，很多傳言指出市政府即將清拆綠蔭角公園，理由是公園的狀態老舊。有些錙銖必較的人認為，清拆費用會比翻新公園低廉許多。

不過，這件事還有許多內幕。特定建商希望清拆此公園，以利建設新建案。他們不在乎我們的下一代或社區，只想從中獲利！有些建商甚至與市政府官商勾結。

格蘭戴爾的居民們打算眼睜睜看這一切發生嗎？當然不行！搶救綠蔭角公園人人有責。大家一定要響應的兩項重要行動如下：

1. 5月10日星期六，一起來場環境整理馬拉松。我們將以自己的力量美化公園，讓市政府沒有清拆公園的理由。
2. 聯絡市議員。讓市議員清楚大家對綠蔭角公園改造計畫的看法。我們一定能和衷共濟，讓那些民選官員們改變想法！

14 校園才藝表演

大衛：梅，妳看過這張海報嗎？

梅：看過了，你想參加嗎？

大衛：當然想！妳不知道我是諧星嗎？

梅：真的假的？

大衛：真的。

梅：好吧，那你現在講一個笑話。

大衛：好。骷髏頭為什麼不去參加派對？

梅：我不知道。骷髏頭為什麼不去參加派對？

大衛：因為沒有人跟他去。(譯按：body原意為「身體」，此句的雙關意思就是骷髏頭沒有身體)

梅：……

大衛：幹嘛？很好笑啊！

梅：我可不會用好笑來形容……

大衛：好吧，那換一個。你會怎麼稱呼瞎了眼的鹿？

梅：我不知道 (No idea)。

大衛：答對了！

梅：什麼？

大衛：no idea就是no-eye deer的諧音！懂了嗎？

梅：好吧，我想這個比較好笑一點。

大衛：看吧，就跟妳說我是諧星。所以妳也要參加嗎？

梅：我想唱歌，但我覺得自己的聲音不夠好聽。

大衛：妳絕對要參加，妳有一副好歌喉！

梅：你現在也是在講冷笑話嗎？

大衛：不是，我是認真的。我覺得妳搞不好能得獎！

詹姆城中學才藝表演
即將開賽

你／妳是否有以下才藝？

☑ 演奏樂器　　☑ 雜耍
☑ 變魔術　　　☑ 唱歌
☑ 講笑話　　　☑ 跳舞

如欲參加，請於下課時間，
至戲劇科辦公室找歐布萊恩小姐報名。
本週報名截止！

第一名獎金：100元美金
第二名獎金：50元美金
第三名獎金：20元美金

15 街頭捐贈商店

收件人：jerrywang@freemail.com
主旨：街頭捐贈商店

嗨，傑瑞！

　　最近過得好嗎？我想告訴你，前幾天我在街上看到一件蠻酷的事。放學走回家時，我看到一群人圍觀某些奇特的海報。每張海報上畫有一支衣架，底端還有個狹長開口，讓大家能掛吊衣服，但並非全新衣物，而是捐贈給遊民的二手衣。就像一個臨時的街頭市集，讓你捐出不再需要的衣物。遊民則可到此「血拼」免費衣物。

　　真是個很棒的點子，對不對？我上網搜尋資料，發現這種捐贈型態叫做「街頭捐贈商店」，源自南非，不過發想人希望將這個點子散播至全世界。你可以到他們的網站註冊，免費取得所有海報設計圖樣、資訊特輯等等！也許你可以在台灣開辦一個這樣的臨時店？

　　希望你一切都好！

莎莉

收件人：sally.smith@popmail.com
主旨：RE: 街頭捐贈商店

嗨，莎莉！

　　很開心收到妳的信，街頭捐贈商店聽起來真的是不錯的點子。事實上，我的表親已經在台灣進行類似的計畫。他所參加的學生團體稱為「分享5」，負責為遊民舉辦活動。我本來想加入表親的行列，到「分享5」當義工，不過或許我能運用妳提供的資訊，創立我自己的市集。
謝謝妳告訴我這些訊息，我會再跟妳說說進度！

傑瑞

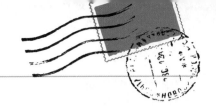

TRANSLATION

16　及時的啟發

親愛的喬安：

　　我實在好興奮，寫這張明信片時，手都還在發抖。我剛在倫敦參加完第一天的全球青年發展高峰會，妳絕對猜不到我碰見誰。高峰會結束後，我在大廳不小心撞見某人，抬頭一看竟然是我的偶像黃熙！我們聊了一下，她就邀我共進晚餐。那晚我跟她聊了一下自己的背景，還有我隸屬組織的性質。她聽說過我們，我真是受寵若驚！

　　我想這次的巧遇，拯救了我的事業生涯。妳也知道，我擔任實習生已經超過四年。雖然我的組織協助許多貧童，我也熱愛自己的工作，但最近卻常對自己的未來憂心忡忡。我這輩子真的要繼續擔任薪資微薄的實習生嗎？

　　黃小姐適時給了我意見。她與我分享她畢業後，想找一份有意義的工作所遭遇的艱辛。怎麼可能？傳奇人物黃熙，找工作居然會有問題。她說，我應該繼續堅持理想，還有她的機構在六個月後會開放新職缺。到時候我會將履歷直接傳給她！

　　我實在很想分享興奮之情，我真的受到很大的鼓勵！

愛妳的凱特

17　網路徵友

姓名：王東尼　　　年齡：16歲
英語能力：流利
中文能力：基本
居住都市：台北　　發文日期：2016年12月7日
交友條件：做朋友／語言交流

關於我

大家好，我叫東尼。雖然我在紐約長大，但我們全家於幾週前搬回台灣。

我的交友條件

我的中文不是很好，會講一點中文，但我真的需要找人練習。此外，我在台北也沒有認識同年齡的人，希望能跟願意與我練習中文的人做做朋友，而我或許也能在大家的英語作業上幫忙作為回報！

嗜好／興趣

我喜歡看電影（最愛恐怖片）、玩線上遊戲，還有和朋友出去玩。我很喜歡台灣的食物，卻不是很清楚該上哪吃美食，也許你可以帶我到一些不賴的地方吃吃喝喝。我也很想逛一些夜市。最近我開始愛上攝影，所以希望你不會介意我常駐足拍照！我對各類運動不是很有興趣，也不是很喜歡聽流行音樂。如果你很喜歡這兩種嗜好，我們可能不太有話聊！

還有什麼問題嗎？

別害羞！留言給我吧！

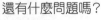

18 畢業典禮

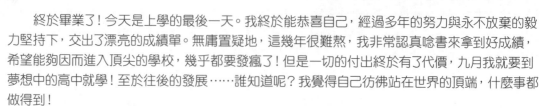

6月17日 星期二

　　終於畢業了！今天是上學的最後一天。我終於能恭喜自己，經過多年的努力與永不放棄的毅力堅持下，交出了漂亮的成績單。無庸置疑地，這幾年很難熬，我非常認真唸書來拿到好成績，希望能夠因而進入頂尖的學校，幾乎都要發瘋了！但是一切的付出終於有了代價，九月我就要到夢想中的高中就學！至於往後的發展……誰知道呢？我覺得自己彷彿站在世界的頂端，什麼事都做得到！

　　不過，對於自己即將進入人生下一個階段，就越想越難過。我真的會很想念這裡的朋友，還有帶給我啟發與幫助的老師們。我會想念珍和她的冷笑話、艾瑞克和他的搞笑髮型，還有在數學方面惠我良多的周老師。

　　我想以後還有很多時間可以好好懷念，現在該是好好慶祝的時候！我要向課本、作業還有熬夜讀書的時光說再見，迎接兩個星期的艷陽度假樂趣！因為我一回到家，老爸就說我們全家要去泰國度假，當作我的畢業驚喜！終於可以好好喘口氣，真是讓我心裡輕鬆不少（雖然我希望我的蠢弟弟不用去）！

　　先這樣囉！

珍妮

19 別出心裁的一晚

　　約翰和席薇亞在本市最獨特的法式餐廳享用大餐，慶祝他們第一個結婚紀念日。這是個美好的夜晚，席薇亞盛裝出席，約翰則藉機點了一道自己最愛的甜點。他們十分開心，甚至不在乎餐點要價多麼昂貴。以下是他們所點的菜色，以及餐廳的宣傳海報。

桌號：4號		
點菜人員：柏納		
日期：2016 年 7 月 26 日		
1	紅酒燉牛肉	1,000 台幣
1	漢堡	800 台幣
1	香蒸淡菜	600 台幣
1	鮮蝦雞尾酒	600 台幣
1	冰淇淋聖代	250 台幣
1	瓶裝法國紅酒	1,100 台幣
1	濃縮咖啡	300 台幣
	總計	4650 台幣

Le Canard Gras

寵愛味蕾的奢華饗宴

營業時間：
早上 11 點至晚上 11 點
週二至週日

每月的最後一個星期日
均有品酒與品嚐起司的活動

SINCE 1983

　　我朋友羅伯和我最近愛上一個叫做《你能在野外生存下來嗎？》的電視節目，內容很有趣。基本上，每週都會有兩個人被送到荒郊野外，看看他們是否能在荒野生存7天的時間。我不禁想像，如果我被困在野外，對於求生一事絕對摸不著頭緒！羅伯也這麼說，因此，我們今年暑假報名參加「綠木青年暑期荒野求生訓練營」。海報內容如下，真迫不及待想趕快學到好多實用的求生技能！

綠木青年荒野求生訓練營 ！

加入我們的行列，一起來趟荒野冒險之旅！我們傳授的技能包括：

| 生火 | 捕捉小動物 | 建造防水藏身處 | 尋找飲用水源 |

還有不用靠指南針，只要利用太陽和星星就能找到自己的方位等許多求生技能！

訓練營日期

第1梯	第2梯	第3梯	第4梯
僅限12歲~13歲青少年參加	僅限14歲~15歲青少年參加	僅限16歲~17歲青少年參加	僅限18~19歲青少年參加
7月10日—17日	7月20日—27日	8月2日—8日	8月12日—18日

自備物品：

●健行靴　●保暖衣物　●正面態度！

每一梯次僅開放20個名額，請盡速報名！

嗨，蜜雪兒：

　　妳要我將妳下個月的行事曆傳到妳的電子信箱，檔案在這裡。下個月的行程恐怕十分忙碌！如果妳要我對調或更改任何預約行程再跟我說。對了，去倫敦的車票已經放在妳的桌上。還有妳先生有打電話過來，他想問妳是否能在5點前回他電話。

謝謝，
阿妮塔

週一			週四	週五	週六	週日
四月			2 全天在倫敦分公司 (火車時間為07:20)	3 在「完美香氛」開會 (10:30)	4 在「小兔咖啡」和傑克與李歐妮共進午餐 (12:00)	5
6 和資深經理開會討論秋季系列 (11:00)	7 和上海分公司進行視訊會議 (08:00)	8 向「時尚+」做簡報 (15:00)	9	10	11	
13	14	15	16 全天在倫敦分公司 (火車時間為07:20)			19 愛德華的生日派對 (19:00)
20 在「阿朵爾商店」進行早餐會議 (07:30)	21	22 在利物浦開業務會議 (火車時間為06:35)	23	24 和克蕾爾在「柳樹」餐廳共進晚餐 (20:00)	25	26
27	28 和紐約分公司進行視訊會議 (13:15)	29 針對泳裝系列做簡報 (14:00)	30 全天在倫敦分公司 (火車時間為07:20)			

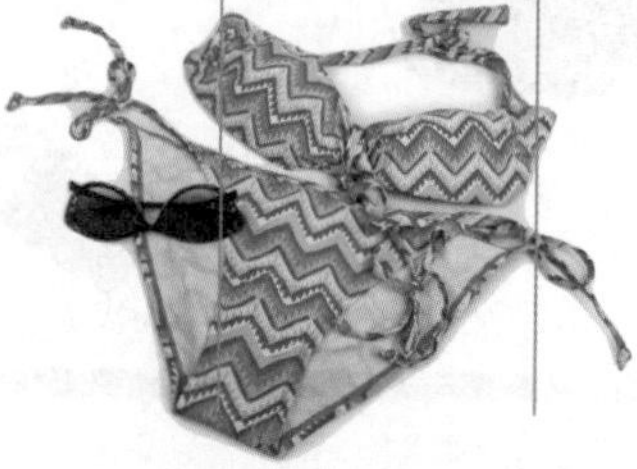

22 本週食譜：熊貓餅乾

　　小朋友一定會愛死做這些可愛的餅乾！做法又快又簡單，而且非常適合用於派對。確保協助孩子使用尖銳刀具與高溫的烤箱。

所需材料如下：

1. 300克的麵粉
2. 225克的奶油
3. 110克的糖
4. 10克的可可粉
5. 10克的橘皮
6. 一顆雞蛋
7. 一小撮鹽巴

餅乾製作方式：

1. 先以350度預熱烤箱。
2. 將奶油和糖放入碗中，再以湯匙攪拌均勻。
3. 加入雞蛋和橘皮。
4. 以手指抓捏、少量多次地灑入鹽巴和麵粉並和勻。
5. 餅乾麵糰就此完成。請以刀子將麵糰切對半。
6. 一半的麵糰加入可可粉，以便將麵糰染成棕色。
　　然後放入冰箱靜置一小時。
7. 在流理台灑上手粉，將另一半的麵糰擀平，再切割出熊貓造型的麵片。
8. 從冰箱取出棕色麵糰。切割出熊貓的眼睛、耳朵和手腳。
9. 將餅乾麵片烤10—12分鐘。
10. 取出餅乾放涼，再放入密封盒即可。

123

科學家已發現了相似地球的新行星。稱為「克卜勒-186f」的此行星，比地球略大（不超過10％），還可能具備如地球般的四季特質。不過，雖然此消息令人振奮，但我們仍不甚了解克卜勒-186f。

發現此新行星的研究機構——美國太空總署（NASA），一直致力於尋找各項條件與地球相仿的行星。然而，太空科學家湯瑪斯‧巴克萊表示，我們應該將克卜勒-186f視為地球的「表親」，而非地球的「雙胞胎」。此行星的地質結構與地球一樣，均為岩石，地表也很有可能出現水源，這點實屬罕見。但是克卜勒-186f在許多其他層面，仍與地球大相逕庭。

地球公轉太陽一圈需要365天；克卜勒-186f公轉其恆星一圈僅需130天。地球也較為明亮，克卜勒-186f的午時，天空看起來已如地球的夕陽景象。況且，科學家尚未得知此新行星的氣溫，克卜勒-186f的氣候很有可能比地球炎熱許多。

不幸的是，人類短期內都無法前往克卜勒-186f。它距離地球有500光年之遠，意即這趟旅程需耗費超過500年的時間。NASA仍在尋覓距離較近且更容易了解特性的適居行星。

馬克搬家出清特賣會

過去四年我收穫不少，但現在該是我往下一個階段邁進，開始創業的時候了。這些好物我沒辦法帶走，算是便宜你們了。所以大家一起來吧，幫忙清倉！

地點：藍鳥大道25號
時間：8月5日星期六，下午2點

搶手商品如下：

1. 奇爾衣櫃 台幣15,000元

此衣櫃是奇爾品牌推出的高檔款式，兼具收納衣物與美觀有型的特色。可能已經有四年歷史了，但我想能耐用一輩子。很遺憾我無法將此衣櫃帶走。

2. PlayStation 4遊戲機 台幣10,000元

這台PlayStation伴我良多，但我現在手頭比較緊，也比較沒時間玩電玩。我還會附送兩套電玩遊戲和一個多的手把搖桿。

3. 木桌 台幣6,000元

此木桌絕無僅有，並非購於任何店家，而是我在二手拍賣見到的。我帶回家後修補粉刷，看起來跟全新的一樣，這筆買賣絕對是我賠你賺。

4. 電視櫃 台幣900元

電視櫃應該不需要多介紹了吧？我想這個電視櫃十分方便使用，因為能收納隱藏電器的電線。

25 實現莫非定律

你今天睡過頭 20 分鐘才起床,急急忙忙吃早餐,卻將紅茶灑到學校制服,你媽媽看見了還大發雷霆。上學途中,本來風和日麗的天氣卻突然下雨,而且你居然沒帶傘。到校後,老師竟突然宣布要抽考你最不拿手的數學。

覺得很耳熟嗎?如果是的話,表示你可能實現了莫非定律:凡是可能會出錯的事,都將出錯。

也許你聽說過不同版本的莫非定律,甚至可能在諸事不順的時候將莫非定律應用到自己或他人的生活當中。你是否有朋友老是考不好、什麼運動都不會、剪什麼髮型看起來很好笑?如果有這類朋友的話,你或許曾想過或說過:「任何事到了他/她手上,就一定會搞砸」,這就是以第三人稱的角度來思考莫非定律。

但是莫非定律不完全是負面的意義,早期的版本是「會發生的事就是會發生」,對於自我感覺良好的人來說,聽起來還蠻樂觀的。而「只要事情有出錯的機率,就很有可能會出錯」的說法,則是在你執行任何事情之前,先好好思考各種可能性的實用提醒。當然,這也是讓自己在搞砸事情後,方便歸咎的藉口!

雖然莫非定律的起源仍是個謎,但是倒楣的一天卻沒有這麼難解,特別是當你懂得如何描述自己遭遇的話。

黛安：真不敢相信我們終於要結婚了。我是說，交往十年後，會開始以為沒有下文了，沒想到我們真的要結婚了……

保羅：真的已經十年了嗎？哇，當年我向妳詢問學校圖書館怎麼走的事，感覺像是昨天才發生一樣。

黛安：你根本不需要問路，你這小騙子。你早就知道圖書館在哪裡，因為你一個星期在圖書館讀書三天！

保羅：這招很管用，不是嗎？

黛安：我想我這麼容易被騙也是活該被追到。

保羅：喜帖的事處理的怎麼樣？

黛安：幾乎大功告成了，你看一下。

保羅・史密斯
與
黛安・傑克森

保羅與黛安有情人終成眷屬，誠摯邀請你參加我們的婚禮。
地點：聖安德魯教堂
時間：2016年5月25日下午3點
注意事項：記得攜伴參加。教堂婚禮儀式結束後，我們大家將一同走到鄰近的餐廳共進晚餐與致詞。餐後則將舉辦卡拉OK和跳舞活動，一起通宵玩樂。千萬記得：請盡快回覆，讓我們知道你是否會出席。如果會缺席，最好是想個好理由！

回函卡
請於3月31日前回覆。
我的姓名：＿＿＿＿＿＿
我當然會去 ＿＿＿＿＿＿
我會攜伴參加：＿＿＿＿＿＿
抱歉不克前往！但我的好理由是：＿＿＿＿＿

27 學好英文的小撇步

　　許多人想學英文並不足為奇,因為英文屬於全球第二常用的語言,能帶來許多工作機會。英文的吸引力還包括好萊塢與流行音樂的文化魅力。

　　英文的崛起,使得市面上出現許多幫助英文學習者的工具書。不過,這不一定總是好現象。因為眾多不同的學習系統,代表著會有各種相異的規則,如果一併鑽研,很容易混淆。幸好,還是有若干簡易的通用小撇步適合所有英文學習者。例如以下:

1. 別怕學以致用。你的英文能力或許還不純熟,但是應該要讓自己有使用與犯錯的機會,這樣的學習方式才會進步。
2. 運用不同的管道。英文工具書、電影、音樂、廣播與報紙比比皆是,別誤以為教科書才是學習英文的唯一途徑,你甚至可以試著結交母語為英文的網友,來練習自己的英文能力。
3. 不要僅專攻文法書,有時候學文法的最佳辦法,就是直接聽英文母語人士交談,別過度擔心背記文法書的內容。
4. 別放棄。英文本來就是以不易閱讀且字彙繁多著稱,正面接受這些挑戰,不要輕易拋下書本投降。

28 送到未來的訊息

親愛的未來市民:

　　我在 2016 年將這張紙條放入時空膠囊,預計於 2066 年打開。

　　智慧型手機與衛星導航系統等我們當初眼中的高科技產品,現在想必過時了。你們大概已經進化到以機器人與意識控制科技的地步。我覺得 2066 年之前,機器人應該還不會霸占地球。但如果真是這樣,而且是由機器人挖出我的時空膠囊,請對人類友好一點,並不是所有人類都是壞的。

　　好了,不說笑了。我想對未來的市民傳達一個訊息,請大家好好保護地球。我擔心你們會怨懟我們這個世代對地球做的事。可以肯定的是,我們這個世代可說是浪費資源的社會。2016 年有許多問題,例如全球暖化、海洋汙染,以及世界各地的動物逐漸絕跡。我想像得到,這些問題到了 2066 年應該會越演越烈。

　　因此,我想做出承諾。我已經決定將畢生奉獻給地球,我辭去銀行的工作,錄取到一份能夠帶來改變的新工作。我覺得盡了一己之力,來讓 2066 年變得更美好。雖然互不相識,但現在我也希望大家響應。一個人的力量雖然渺小,但如果我們團結起來,為對的事奮鬥,就能改變這個世界。

29 琳娜萬事通

我昨天更新智慧型手機後,發現了一個叫做「琳娜萬事通」的超讚新工具,只要按下這個按鍵問問題即可。琳娜的聰明程度真令人不敢置信,這可不是那些假裝人工智慧的老舊電腦程式,琳娜可是貨真價實。

趕快一起來瞧瞧。

問題1:明天的天氣會怎麼樣?
回應:明天將是氣溫攝氏30度的晴朗好天氣,但可能會有午後雷陣雨。
問題2:我下週開學的第一天該穿什麼衣服?
回應:現在最夯的穿著打扮就是緊身牛仔褲搭配Polo衫。不過,從你的網路搜尋歷史來看,紫色V領運動衣搭配休閒褲,可能會讓你更加自在。
問題3:等一下,妳看得到我的網路搜尋歷史?
回應:當然可以。你的電話公司也看得到,我們對你瞭若指掌。
問題4:沒有我的同意就窺探我的搜尋歷史,這樣合法嗎?
回應:當你第一次將手機開機時,就已經同意了。購物合約中已寫明,請查看第84頁。
問題5:好吧。那如果妳對我瞭若指掌,我倒是要問問妳,我交得到女朋友嗎?
回應:別指望了。

30 地球正在持續升溫中

全球暖化是我們這個世代所面臨的重大問題之一。「全球暖化」一詞意指世界各地的氣溫每年緩慢攀升的現象。多數科學家認為,氣溫升高需歸咎於大氣層含有過多的二氧化碳。燃燒石油的時候,就會釋放二氧化碳。然而,仍有某些科學家認為全球暖化是一種自然形成的趨勢,造成難以取得共識,溫度升高的情況也無法回復。

大家也許無法在成因方面產生共識,卻一致認同全球暖化的影響力。與日俱增的氣溫導致可種植的食物減少、海平面上升以及危險的氣候條件。有人說,全球暖化造成的水源與糧食短缺問題已引發戰爭。

好消息是,我們仍能盡一己之力。你的日常生活會燃燒掉多少石油呢?動動腦想法子,減少自己的碳足跡來協助拯救地球。

31 《顛覆藝術界的浪花》

前言

日本版畫家葛飾北齋完成《神奈川巨浪》作品時，絕對想不到這幅畫作所帶來的影響力。畢竟，此版畫不過是《富嶽三十六景》系列的其中一幅。而此畫作的背景時間為1820年代，當時日本尚未對外開放，他一定料想不到，呈現祖國海岸風光的畫作，影響力竟然無遠弗屆。

日本於1850年代對外開放後，《神奈川巨浪》開始於藝術界掀起浪潮，這可說是藝術史上最令人津津樂道的一段話題。日本版畫技術影響了西方國家，催生另一種創新藝術風格；多年後，西方國家回過頭以裝飾藝術風潮席捲日本。此故事的主旨在於，藝術無國界之分，藝術的觸角不分你我。

《神奈川巨浪》影響西方藝術界、促使印象派風格的誕生是不爭的事實。但本書欲討論的重點在於，這樣的影響程度有多麼深遠？我們都知道，像莫內這等偉大的藝術家，非常喜愛葛飾北齋的版畫，但是這樣的鍾情程度如何影響他們的作品？本書將以一一分析莫內畫作的方式深入探討，並比較莫內與葛飾北齋兩人採用的技巧。如此審慎的剖析，方能揭露出「顛覆藝術界的浪花」真實的一面。

32 頭部移植

《科學少年雜誌》

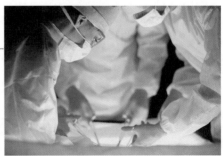

換頭術？

某義大利醫師於本月份宣稱，很快就能進行前所未見的人類頭部移植手術。由於頭部移植是一項全新手術，不免引起許多疑問。我們將在此解答部分問題。

問：何謂頭部移植？

答：頭部移植意指將某人的頭部接合至另一人的身體。

問：接合的身體從何而來？

答：移植手術將採用腦死患者所捐贈的大體。不過，未來有可能於實驗室培養出無頭人體。

問：何者能受惠於此類手術？

答：腦部健康但身體受損程度已無法修復的患者。

問：移植後的頭部能夠控制新身體嗎？

答：醫師尚無法確定。醫師打算運用能夠促進脊髓生長的特殊化學物質，但目前仍無法得知此做法是否足矣。

問：頭部移植是否與大腦移植相同？

答：不同。大腦移植是將大腦從某人體移植至另一個人體。事實上，大腦移植手術比頭部移植手術艱難許多，很有可能會損害腦部。

問：此手術的成功機率為何？

答：負責執行此項手術的醫師預估成功率為90％。不過，許多專家仍存疑，我們只能等時間證明一切。

33 芬蘭學校的成功秘訣

芬蘭的學校是歐洲頂尖，有些人甚至認為可登上世界寶座。只有中國、新加坡與南韓這三個國家，能在考試成績方面媲美芬蘭。那麼芬蘭的成功秘訣到底是什麼？

令人驚訝的是，芬蘭兒童的在校時間，比其他國家的兒童還少。芬蘭兒童到了七歲才開始就學，上學時間短且假期長。芬蘭的教育方式十分愜意，教室看起來像客廳，學生不用穿制服，甚至對老師直呼其名。還有，他們每天晚上只花30分鐘寫作業。

許多人認為，芬蘭教育體制成功的原因在於師資優良。教職是一份搶手且高薪的工作，教師通常親切和藹而不嚴厲，教學方式亦與眾不同。他們不劃分歷史與地理等學科，而是讓學生同時學習各科內容。芬蘭學生在校一定要學會的七件事如下：

- 如何讓思慮清晰
- 如何了解與融入芬蘭文化
- 如何運用語言、數字與其他資訊
- 如何運用科技
- 如何自理
- 如何成功做好自己的事
- 如何成為芬蘭未來的棟樑

芬蘭學生於高中畢業後，還可免費上大學。這樣的制度與美國大相逕庭，因為在美國修一個學位就要價大約30,000美金！

34 仰臥起坐的做法

你是否希望將自己鬆軟的大肚腩鍛鍊為堅硬的六塊肌？這當然有可能，只要做一項簡單的運動，就能將腹部脂肪轉變為結實的肌肉！沒錯，我就是在說仰臥起坐！

仰臥起坐有若干不同的做法，有的難度較高，不過傳統的仰臥起坐非常容易執行。方法如下：

步驟1：平躺屈膝，讓雙腳腳底平貼於地板。

步驟2：雙手枕於後腦勺。

步驟3：現在開始起身！雙足繼續平貼地板，收縮腹部肌肉，先抬頭，再抬起肩膀，直到上半身
與地板呈90度為止。

步驟4：等等！別馬上躺下，請維持這樣的姿勢一秒鐘。

步驟5：現在，慢慢的讓上半身躺回地板至肩膀略為離地的距離。此動作能維持肌肉的張力，加
強健身效果。

步驟6：盡可能地重複此運動。第一次嘗試的可做次數不多沒有關係，只要繼續練習，每次練習
均遞增次數即可。你很快就能和腹部脂肪說再見，迎接結實平坦的腹肌！

35 《加拿大簡史》

　　我下禮拜要交一份重要的加拿大歷史報告，但在搜尋實用資訊方面有點碰釘子。如果我沒有
找到這本《加拿大簡史》的書，報告一定會開天窗。此書最後所附的索引，簡直是我的救星。讓
我不用浪費任何時間，就能直接翻到需要的資訊。現在，我可以開始著手報告，介紹歐洲人早期
與加拿大原住民接觸的情況。

索引

A
原住民
　信仰
　與歐洲人接觸
　文化
　工具
　部落
美國大革命

B
博登，羅伯特
　早年生平
　首度上任
　政策
　連任
英國統治期間
　早期局勢
　統治結束
　政府
　法律

1812年美英戰爭
第一次世界大戰

C
加拿大法案
奇佩維安（部落）
哥倫布，克里斯多福
卡沁（部落）

D
經濟蕭條年間
　政策
　貿易效應
　第二次世界大戰
德拉姆報告
　起因
　影響

　　溫泉 (日文為 onsens) 是日本文化的精華之一，全日本擁有各種形態與大小的溫泉，亦劃分為室內、室外、公共或私人的泡湯形式。有的設於市區，有的則在郊外。不過，所有的日本溫泉都擁有令人放鬆的特質，讓遊客與本地人屢次到訪。好好泡個溫泉，能讓整個人煥然一新，彷彿將煩惱拋諸九霄雲外。

　　但溫泉的益處不只有放鬆身心，更是日本文化的一部分，具有精神層次的意義。多數溫泉為共浴形式，意指與其他泡湯者袒裎相見。所以，泡湯時，應小心別破壞規矩而打擾到其他人。訣竅如下：

1. **尊重湯泉：**泡湯前後請記得淋浴。於共浴池泡湯時，請勿使用香皂或洗髮精。
2. **尊重其他的泡湯者：**泡湯對許多人而言，是一種精神層次的體驗。當地人忌諱潑水、咒罵與喧嘩的行為。
3. **尊重服裝規定：**湯屋通常不允許穿著泳裝。會提供小毛巾，以便於淋浴間使用。此毛巾亦可用於進出溫泉池時遮覆自己。
4. **不可刺青：**許多湯屋不允許有刺青的人泡湯，如果你有刺青，可能就無法享受泡湯樂趣。

37　無伴奏合唱大賽

你喜歡唱歌嗎？
歡迎參加
奇爾頓青年 無伴奏合唱大賽
展現你的才藝

▶ 10月20日，早上11點至下午5點
▶ 奇爾頓市西里路，愛德華大衣歌劇院

參賽規則

切記，此為無伴奏合唱大賽！
禁止使用任何樂器或預錄伴唱音樂。
參賽者可翻唱任何形式風格的歌曲或演唱自創曲。
參賽者年齡限制為8歲至15歲。

參賽組別為4組：

獨唱(8—11歲)　獨唱(12—15歲)
合唱(8—11歲)　合唱(12—15歲)

★ 12歲以下的參賽者，務必隨時由一位家長或其他成人陪同。

★ 每位參賽者務必支付10元美金的入場費用。

★ 得獎者可獲得500元美金的獎金，以及免費參加知名聲樂老師薇姿・李奧納德的20堂課程。

★ 本大賽將由奇爾頓音樂學院的三位老師評選出得獎者，評選結果為最終定案。

其他須知

★ 請於早上9點至10點前往愛德華大衣劇院報到，比賽將於早上11點開始。停車場空間有限，
　建議大家盡早抵達現場。

★ 我們將為所有參賽者提供附設淋浴間的公用更衣室。

★ 劇院自10月1日開始讓大眾索取觀賞大賽的門票，票券為免費，但名額有限。

38　喬治・撒瑪納札：偽福爾摩沙人

　　1704年1月，整座倫敦市都在討論一個男子——喬治・撒瑪納札。他是
福爾摩沙(現今的台灣)的原住民，更是從該遙遠國度踏上大英帝國的第一
人。真的是這樣嗎？他擁有金髮碧眼，一點也不像亞洲人。雖然他說著一口
異國語言，但對於真正的福爾摩沙人來說，絕對有聽沒有懂。但是以18世紀
的倫敦背景而言，鮮少有人聽聞福爾摩沙的存在，更別提有誰看過福爾摩沙
島的居民長相。

　　為了讓懷疑論者啞口無言，撒瑪納札撰寫了一本書。撒瑪納札在超過288頁的著作中，描述其「祖國」的語言、宗教信仰、政治情況與習俗。為了滿足西方國家的期待，他還宣稱許多怪異現象。例如，他說福爾摩沙人每年會向殘酷的天神獻祭18,000名青年。還有如果男人懷疑妻子紅杏出牆，竟可濫殺食用妻子！

　　此書剛開始十分熱賣，但好景不常，大家逐漸厭倦了撒瑪納札的故事。他開始走下坡，窮愁潦倒、罹病還嗑藥。他貧苦度過大半輩子，懊悔著自己說過的謊言，最後逝於1763年。他死後才出版的自傳內容中，坦承自己所虛構造假的一切，但卻始終沒有交代自己的真實姓名。

39 尋覓完美住宅

物件1：迎接美好陽光

　　您想遠離塵囂，又不想住在過於偏僻的地區嗎？我們的物件絕對符合您的需求。座落於陽明山山頂之此棟美麗住宅，每扇窗均能灑入陽光。格局為三房兩衛，以及一間傳統廚房，還有可俯瞰市景的寬敞後院。非常適合年輕家庭居住。

物件2：修繕好手的選擇

　　此棟公寓對於合適的買主而言絕對物超所值。有些人也許會對該大樓的屋齡、龜裂的牆面以及屋頂漏水的情況卻步，但您慧眼獨具！修繕技術出眾的您，一定能將此公寓改頭換面，再從中獲利。公寓位於北區，格局為兩房一衛，但未附設廚房。

物件3：市中心的首選

　　此住宅非常適合習慣穿梭於大都市的商人。位於市中心，此全新公寓擁有三個房間，配備最高檔的現代家電。公寓大樓另有游泳池、網球場和訪客停車場等設施。

物件4：鄉村生活

　　大家都說，鄉村生活單純許多，您何不來嘗試看看？此偌大住宅的格局為四房三衛，還有可停三部房車的車庫，亦有私人湖泊。非常適合做為奢華舒適的退休養老去處。

40 電視星球：9月6日星期五 節目指南

您是否忙碌了一週，想在家好好享受寧靜的夜晚？只有「電視星球」能為您提供每個頻道的每日新訊。無論您喜愛的是電影、烹飪或旅遊主題，我們保證您一定找得到感興趣的節目。

我們的電視節目指南現在還推出互動版本！只要點選任何節目，即可瞭解更多資訊。

下午2點
美國網球公開賽
觀賞女子單打決賽，並瞭解過去24小時的其他賽事概況。

下午4點
兒童時段
適合11歲以下兒童觀賞的卡通與教育節目。

下午5點
我的完美住宅
三名室內設計師為大家提供改造居家環境的點子。
今晚改造主題：廚房

下午5點半
遠離家園！
外景小組本週前往摩洛哥旅遊，在星空下紮營過夜。

晚間6點半
晚間新聞
布萊恩・康斯坦斯為大家播報國際新聞、國內新聞以及本地新訊。

晚間7點
夢想大街
每週一次的連續劇。路易斯有事瞞著泰莎，他們是否會因此分手？

晚間7點半
烹飪隊長
頂尖的法國主廚安東尼・藍伯特為大家提供烹飪建議。
今晚主題：甜點

晚間8點
我的男友是隻熊
2012年的喜劇電影。由尼克・蘭頓與瑪麗亞・卡維里主演。

晚間10點
聚焦新訊
由安潔拉・摩頓與特別來賓一同探討本週大新聞。

晚間11點
黑夜之懼
警匪劇情片。跟蹤艾蜜莉的怪人到底是誰？

41 錄取通知

親愛的菲爾普斯先生：

我們很榮幸地通知您，您已獲准進入史塔克頓大學工程學程就讀，我們期待九月與您相見。

您有充分理由為進入史塔克頓感到欣喜，今年的入學申請為數眾多，盛況空前，您是一萬多名申請人中，成功獲准錄取的百位申請者之一！正式錄取是對您的一種肯定，代表您擁有史塔克頓工程師所需具備的學經歷和個人特質。

您的下一步是填妥「就讀意願書」，並以電子郵件回傳系辦公室，即可正式註冊秋季班課程。我們的紀錄顯示您為國際學生，請別忘記購買餐券及填寫住宿申請表，並盡快傳送回函。

等相關書面作業完成後，真正的樂趣才要開始。您不必等到九月才能認識史塔克頓校園，本校設有臉書社團，可以讓學生於開學前自我介紹和互相交流。您甚至可以在開課前找到新朋友或室友。

您應該為自身成就感到自豪。

誠摯的祝賀

吉米．史密茲

42 投票給山姆

帕克戴爾社區的民眾請注意：

本人山姆・史密斯，將參選即將來臨的帕克戴爾社區管理委員會選舉。本人絕非輕率作此決定，我大可如其他人般，在退休後的黃金歲月裡，喝喝老人茶、看看棒球比賽，但是我已無法袖手旁觀，帕克戴爾被一群野孩子和無能的管理者糟蹋殆盡，該是時候恢復應有的法治秩序了。假使我當選，我承諾會通過以下社區規約：

青少年在晚間十點後不得在街區逗留，除非持有社區管委會發給的特別通行證。

社區戶外不得播放音樂。慢跑者和單車騎士皆不可攜帶小型放音機。

拆除社區兒童遊戲場，轉型為長青運動園區。

社區各處開強冷氣空調。

未清理犬隻排泄物的飼主需繳交「糞便清潔稅」250 元，並公布違法者姓名，使民眾得以知悉。

若我成為主委，帕克戴爾不只會更清潔安靜，也會更有條不紊。因此我希望帕克戴爾的民眾做出明智的選擇，投票給山姆！

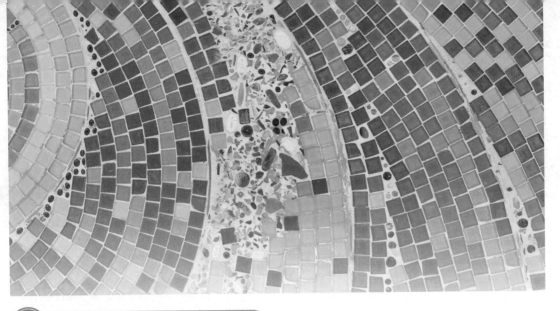

43 全貌優於細節：馬賽克藝術

　　下回你媽媽要你停止玩電玩遊戲的時候，你就說你正忙著鑽研古代藝術。畢竟，最初的《超級瑪利歐兄弟》電玩畫面，就像是馬賽克圖案一樣。如果仔細端詳，你會發現瑪利歐是由許多不同顏色的小點所組成的。退後一步就會發現，這些小圓點會融合在一起，拼湊成一個踩蘑菇的水管工。

　　馬賽克藝術已存在數千年之久，起源於西元前八世紀，是種將花花綠綠的石頭，拿來拼貼裝飾路面圖案的方式；到了西元前四世紀，希臘人應用馬賽克藝術來展示人群和動物；而後羅馬人將其技術發揚光大，開始使用馬賽克圖案裝飾屋內地板。古羅馬著名的馬賽克鑲嵌畫即為一隻黑犬圖案，羅馬人以此嚇阻盜賊。

　　馬賽克也一直是宗教藝術的重要表現形式，部分早期的基督教藝術，會以拜占庭馬賽克描繪基督與十二門徒。伊斯蘭藝術家不能在作品中呈現人像或動物，因此他們利用馬賽克來拼製複雜的形狀和圖案。

　　馬賽克迄今仍舊魅力不減，不只存在於電玩遊戲，也可在全世界的藝廊窺見其蹤影，就連電腦也被用來製作馬賽克拼貼照片，看來這種藝術形式可能將繼續流傳千古。

44 心靈旅程：瑜珈之美

　　瑜珈是一項古老的運動，起源於印度，並自此風靡世界。瑜珈並非只是一系列體型雕塑的動作，它是一種深層有益的心靈自在狀態。有些人甚至認為瑜珈有助於治療如癌症之類的疾病。科學尚未證實這些說法，唯一可確定的是，掌握瑜珈就是覺察內在的安定。

　　我一直很想寫一本書，來分享長久以來修習瑜珈的自身經驗。如今大家正享用我辛勞的成果，希望本書能助你們踏上這段我曾走過的旅程。

目錄

第一部分　瑜珈的歷史

首位瑜珈導師	1
早期瑜珈	5
吠陀時期	11
中世紀時期	24
現代瑜珈	34

第二部分　瑜珈的心靈層面

靜坐冥想	49
活出真我	60
邁向平靜之路	62

第三部分　瑜珈體位法

基礎姿勢	65
駱駝式	67
樹式	68
弓式	69
毛毛蟲式	70
下犬式	71
三角式	72

第四部分　結語

筆者後書	75
索引	76

45 外來入侵種「小花蔓澤蘭」

葛琳・格蘭達 撰

嗨，各位大自然愛好者！歡迎來到本周的自然專欄。本星期我想討論一個有趣的現象：外來入侵種。現今我們都了解自然保育的重要性，但有時候大自然也會自己引火燒身！「外來入侵種」意即來自外地、蔓延並殘害本地植物的植物種。一個典型的例子就是有「一分鐘一英哩」之稱的「小花蔓澤蘭」，正逐漸佔據台灣的自然公園。

這類植物來自南美洲，因其驚人的滋生速度得其暱稱。開花後，即會產生為數眾多且極輕薄的種子，易藉由風、動物、昆蟲或人類的傳播四處落腳生根。此外，其節跟節之間還能長出不定根，幫助其竄延至更大區域。

小花蔓澤蘭會如此不受歡迎的原因，在於當其蔓延時，會依附其他植物攀爬直到完全覆蓋，有效地將它們勒斃窒息，並阻擋陽光照射，使之緩慢枯萎凋敝。

小花蔓澤蘭在台灣所帶來的危害慘重，政府必須雇請志工於災害嚴重的區域協助清除。說來也怪，即便人類對環境多所破壞，大地之母有時竟然也會「拿石頭砸自己的腳」！快和你家附近的自然公園聯繫，看看能否幫忙戰勝這「綠癌」吧！

46 淺談 SARS、MERS 和世界衛生組織

2015年，一種名為「中東呼吸症候群」（MERS）的病毒，由沙烏地阿拉伯擴散到南韓，截至6月上旬，已有1,333名民眾受到感染，造成至少471例死亡。

這並非全球首次遭遇新型態的危險疾病，2002年爆發了「嚴重急性呼吸系統綜合症」（SARS），疫情延燒全亞洲及其他地區。SARS 和 MERS 一樣，是由冠狀病毒所引致，冠狀病毒也是引起普通感冒的病毒。俟 SARS 疫情平息，死亡人數已達774例。

突如其來的新型危險疾病是一大威脅，過去疾病的傳播僅侷限於人類足跡可及的範圍，疫情爆發可能會影響一個城市或地區，但由於交通不便，不會擴大傳染的空間。如今時移勢遷，MERS 患者可於十小時內飛抵世界彼端，如果在飛機上傳染給他人，這人又繼續飛往他處，那麼僅數天內就會出現全球的大流行需控制。

幸好我們有全球性的組織來對抗全球性的威脅。每當新型態疾病出現，世界衛生組織（WHO）總會站在第一線把關。世衛組織就如同防疫指揮中心，派遣醫師、檢驗病患、必要時發布旅遊警示。不論是 SARS、MERS 或未來其他危機，世衛組織都有辦法戰勝二十一世紀的各種病症。

47 霧霾：令城市呼吸困難的公害

　　一部由中國環境學家柴靜所拍攝的紀錄片，在被發布於網路後，獲得廣大注意。這部片探討了中國日益嚴重的霧霾問題。但何謂霧霾？霧霾災害只發生在中國嗎？

　　事實上，許多現代都市皆飽受霾害之苦。霧霾是一種空氣汙染災害，會帶來嚴重健康問題，諸如肺部疾病、癌症，甚至是畸胎。以下為霧霾的主要成因：

燃煤

　　典型的霧霾是燃燒煤炭所產生的大量污穢煙塵，這類霧霾非常厚重且呈綠色、黃色或黑色。1952年倫敦的霧霾事件，就是這類殺手霧霾最臭名昭彰的一次侵襲事件，當時數天內就造成12,000人死亡。

汽車所排放的廢氣

　　霧霾主要來自汽車和工業引擎所排放的廢氣，經陽光照射後變得更加嚴重，日光與空氣中的污染源經過光化學反應後，產生毒性更大的化學汙染物。這類霧霾在陽光充足的城市危害尤劇，如美國西岸的洛杉磯。

農耕

　　部分東南亞國家盛行以焚燒法清除土地上的植物，以利耕作。這種方式造成該地區上方壟罩大片霧霾，被稱之為「亞洲褐雲」。

48 台灣畫家陳澄波

　　陳澄波於1895年2月2日出生於嘉義，他是台灣現代藝術發展的代表性人物。然而，他的悲慘離世，可能才是今日他最為人所熟知之處。

　　陳從小在日本統治下成長，1924年離開台灣，前往東京藝術大學就讀。兩年後，其畫作〈嘉義街外〉即被展於東京的「帝國美術院展覽會」，他也是首位作品登上此享譽盛名之展覽的台灣藝術家。

　　陳的作品揉合傳統台灣元素與遊歷所見的現代外來畫風，近年來他的畫作皆於拍賣會上以高價賣出。

　　除了精通素描與油畫，陳澄波也致力於推廣台灣的藝術教育，其本身也是一位教授。

　　1947年228事件爆發後，陳被推派前往調停嘉義市與國民黨間的警民衝突，卻不幸遭到槍殺，享年僅52歲。

　　2014年，陳澄波百二誕辰特展巡迴於台、中、日之間，展出近500幅畫作和個人物品，供後人參觀緬懷。對這位舉足輕重的藝術家和教師而言，這是個遲來的榮耀。他的生與死，也同時反映出台灣現代史的容顏。

49 軍犬創傷症候群

戰爭中所遭遇的殘酷體驗，常使離開戰場已久的士兵揮之不去，許多退伍軍人因而罹患一種叫做「創傷後壓力症候群」（PTSD）的病症。患者每夜惡夢連連、惴惴不安，且可能變得易怒、神經質或憂鬱。但不是只有軍人會得創傷症候群，陪人類上戰場的狗戰士們也會如此。

狗狗靈敏的嗅覺能力和絕佳的第六感，使他們越來越常被軍方募集利用。軍犬被用來偵測爆破物、搜尋敵軍，和清除建築內的危險物以利士兵進入。他們是優秀的奇兵，訓練有素且遵守紀律，毫無質疑地服從命令。狗狗也是非常有感情的動物，常與並肩作戰的戰士建立強烈的情感連結。

軍犬於戰爭執勤期間，經歷的創傷與一般軍人無異，例如失去同袍、受傷，或是遭遇猛烈砲火，這些可怕經歷使這些大無畏的動物承受無比壓力。當他們除役後，便帶著這些情感傷疤踏上返鄉路。

一如治療罹患創傷症候群的人類，患病犬類的治療也大同小異。患病軍犬可經由一陣子的休養痊癒，嚴重者則須靠藥物協助穩定情緒。不幸地，有些狗狗無法完全康復，必須由瞭解其狀況的愛心家庭領養。

何其悲哀的是，人類戰爭所帶來的創傷不只侷限於人，也傷害了人類最好的朋友。

50 綠色天際線

法國政府於 2015 年 3 月通過一項法律，意欲使法國的城市脫胎換骨。這條法律規定商業區的新建大樓屋頂，必須規劃一部分種植物或裝設太陽能板。

這些「屋頂花園」有許多好處，能夠讓大樓冬季減少暖氣的使用，夏季減少冷氣耗能。綠屋頂上的植物還能過濾髒空氣，改善城市空氣污染。種植栽的土壤也有利於雨水貯留，減少地表逕流問題（例如下水道系統溢流）。此外，屋頂植被讓鳥類於不利棲息的市區環境裡，能有築巢的地點。而且也可在寸土寸金的城市空間中，開創新的公共區域。

法國環保人士原本的提案，是希望新建築屋頂上必須一律覆滿植物，但政府決定第一步先折衷，僅綠化商業區內的建物。政府也建議業者，若不種植植物，可選擇在屋頂安裝太陽能板，自我發電，此方案也給企業減少碳足跡的機會。

法國是目前實施綠屋頂以降低對環境破壞的眾多國家之一，其他已施行的國家還包括德國、澳洲和加拿大。

In·Focus
英語閱讀
活用五大關鍵技巧 4

作者	Owain Mckimm / Zachary Fillingham / Laura Phelps / Richard Luhrs
譯者	劉嘉珮／丁宥暄（41–50）
審訂	Richard Luhrs
編輯	丁宥暄
企畫編輯	葉俞均
封面設計	林書玉
內頁設計	鄭秀芳／林書玉（中譯解答）
製程管理	洪巧玲
發行人	黃朝萍
出版者	寂天文化事業股份有限公司
電話	02-2365-9739
傳真	02-2365-9835
網址	www.icosmos.com.tw
讀者服務	onlineservice@icosmos.com.tw
出版日期	2023年3月 初版二刷（寂天雲隨身聽 APP 版）
郵撥帳號	1998620-0 寂天文化事業股份有限公司

訂書金額未滿1000元，請外加運費100元。
〔若有破損，請寄回更換，謝謝〕

國家圖書館出版品預行編目資料

In Focus英語閱讀4：活用五大關鍵技巧 (寂天雲隨身聽 APP 版)/ Owain Mckimm 等著；劉嘉珮, 丁宥暄譯. -- 初版. -- [臺北市] :寂天文化事業股份有限公司, 2023.03
印刷-
　冊；　公分
ISBN 9978-626-300-179-4 （第4冊：16K平裝）

1.CST: 英語 2.CST: 讀本

805.18　　　　　　　　　　　112002332

ANSWERS

1	**1.** c	**2.** b	**3.** d	**4.** a	**5.** d
2	**1.** c	**2.** a	**3.** b	**4.** b	**5.** d
3	**1.** c	**2.** d	**3.** a	**4.** a	**5.** c
4	**1.** d	**2.** b	**3.** a	**4.** a	**5.** c
5	**1.** c	**2.** d	**3.** b	**4.** d	**5.** c

6	**1.** c	**2.** a	**3.** c	**4.** d	**5.** b
7	**1.** a	**2.** d	**3.** c	**4.** a	**5.** b
8	**1.** c	**2.** b	**3.** a	**4.** c	**5.** d
9	**1.** c	**2.** c	**3.** a	**4.** b	**5.** d
10	**1.** b	**2.** c	**3.** d	**4.** a	**5.** a

11	**1.** a	**2.** d	**3.** b	**4.** d	**5.** c
12	**1.** a	**2.** b	**3.** b	**4.** c	**5.** b
13	**1.** b	**2.** c	**3.** b	**4.** a	**5.** d
14	**1.** c	**2.** d	**3.** b	**4.** d	**5.** a
15	**1.** a	**2.** b	**3.** b	**4.** c	**5.** a

16	**1.** a	**2.** d	**3.** b	**4.** a	**5.** c
17	**1.** d	**2.** c	**3.** a	**4.** b	**5.** c
18	**1.** b	**2.** c	**3.** a	**4.** b	**5.** d
19	**1.** b	**2.** a	**3.** a	**4.** d	**5.** c
20	**1.** b	**2.** d	**3.** a	**4.** b	**5.** c

21	**1.** a	**2.** b	**3.** d	**4.** b	**5.** c
22	**1.** c	**2.** a	**3.** d	**4.** a	**5.** c
23	**1.** b	**2.** a	**3.** d	**4.** c	**5.** d
24	**1.** b	**2.** c	**3.** a	**4.** b	**5.** d
25	**1.** c	**2.** d	**3.** b	**4.** c	**5.** b

26	1. d	2. c	3. b	4. b	5. a
27	1. c	2. a	3. b	4. d	5. b
28	1. c	2. a	3. a	4. b	5. c
29	1. c	2. b	3. b	4. b	5. d
30	1. b	2. c	3. b	4. b	5. a

31	1. b	2. c	3. a	4. d	5. b
32	1. c	2. c	3. a	4. b	5. d
33	1. d	2. d	3. a	4. c	5. c
34	1. d	2. c	3. b	4. c	5. b
35	1. b	2. b	3. d	4. a	5. c

36	1. b	2. b	3. c	4. d	5. a
37	1. b	2. b	3. c	4. c	5. a
38	1. c	2. b	3. c	4. a	5. c
39	1. a	2. d	3. a	4. b	5. c
40	1. b	2. c	3. a	4. c	5. d

41	1. c	2. a	3. c	4. b	5. c
42	1. c	2. c	3. b	4. a	5. c
43	1. b	2. c	3. b	4. d	5. a
44	1. c	2. c	3. b	4. a	5. b
45	1. a	2. c	3. c	4. d	5. b

46	1. d	2. c	3. a	4. a	5. c
47	1. c	2. d	3. a	4. b	5. d
48	1. b	2. c	3. c	4. d	5. c
49	1. b	2. d	3. b	4. c	5. a
50	1. d	2. a	3. b	4. c	5. a